WHERE ONE MAN STANDS

The brothers had never been close —
until a killer cut down their father at
the end of the long trail drive. That
was the day their world would change
forever. Side by side they set out to
battle the killer they hunted and the
murderous desert. Until that day and
hour when they faced their man, not
as enemies but as true brothers with
but a single thought. Revenge or death!
They would accept nothing less —
together.

CHAD HAMMER

WHERE ONE MAN STANDS

Complete and Unabridged

LINFORD
Leicester

First published in Great Britain in 2007 by
Robert Hale Limited
London

First Linford Edition
published 2009
by arrangement with
Robert Hale Limited
London

British Library CIP Data

Hammer, Chad
    Where one man stands.—Large print ed.—
Linford western library
1. Western stories
2. Large type books
I. Title
823.9'14 [F]

ISBN 978–1–84782–508–7

Published by
F. A. Thorpe (Publishing)
Anstey, Leicestershire

Set by Words & Graphics Ltd.
Anstey, Leicestershire
Printed and bound in Great Britain by
T. J. International Ltd., Padstow, Cornwall

This book is printed on acid-free paper

1

The Brothers

It was noon as the two men rode slowly down the main street of Wolflock.

They passed by the long-fronted store and the ruins of a building with the word 'Marshal' in faded letters above the door. They paused to examine a laden buckboard standing before the livery stables, then, exchanging brief words, the riders moved on to rein in at the Bird Cage, Wolflock's only saloon.

From the shade of the saloon porch overhang a loafer in faded denim studied them idly as they dismounted. He ran an appraising eye over the sturdy horses and the two riders caked in trail dust. They were young men, one tall and the other of medium height, both with the bronzed skin of men who lived their lives in the open. The smaller man was slim with black hair and an Indian's grace in his walk. His companion was tall and fair with broad shoulders and flashing white teeth.

'Texas!' so the lounger decided. 'You can never mistake a man from Texas. They all git around like they own the whole dad-blamed country and any place else worth the ownin'.'

The man spat dispiritedly into the dust as the newcomers mounted the worn steps and crossed the porch to disappear through the batwings.

Coming in from the glare of the street, it took some time to accustom the eyes to the gloom of the saloon. It was pleasantly cool indoors with all windows but one shuttered against the heat. The single open window at the far end of the bar offered escape for the eternal tobacco smoke and afforded drinkers a view of a littered back alley.

The newcomers idly appraised the Bird Cage's clientele. Some half-dozen dusty cowhands lounged against the bar and a sharp-eyed faro player was dealing himself solitaire near the doors. In back four men sat absorbed in a blackjack game.

'There he is,' murmured the taller rider, jerking a thumb at a rawboned figure sucking desperately on a hand-made cigarette at a corner of the bar.

His companion grunted and they strolled across to the bar, spurs jingling softly.

As they approached, the man turned. Slowly his bleary gaze focused and a flicker of apprehension crossed his face, only to give way immediately to a gap-toothed beam of welcome.

'Ryan and Matt Freeman!' he roared. 'Tarnation! Just imagine running into you two fellers here. What in Jehosephat are you doing away from the herd — your pappy fire you, mebbe? Haw! Haw! But come on, join old Cobby in a drink, huh? Barman! Hey, yeah you, Billy. Two clean glasses, pronto, quick smart . . . and at the goddamn double!'

He was overdoing the glad-handed

greeting by a long horse mile. The face of the dark-headed Matt Freeman remained blank as he lifted the bottle from the bartop. Barely two inches of golden liquor remained. His dark eyes drilled at their cowhand.

'What's the idea, Cobb?' he demanded without raising his voice.

'What ya mean, Matt boy?' the man replied, eyes innocently wide. 'Just washing down a little trail dust is all. No law against that now, is there?'

The barman placed two shot glasses on the bar and reached for the bottle to pour.

'No, hold it,' said Matt Freeman.

He turned back to Cobb. When he spoke now his voice had an edge to it. 'You were sent here to town last night just to get supplies. But we had to come in looking for you today, and then we find you drunk.'

The cowboy managed to look both innocent and offended at the one time.

'Drunk? Who's drunk? I can hold my liquor better than any man I know!' As

4

he spoke he snapped ramrod erect and inflated his chest, but ruined the effect by listing noticeably to one side.

Intimidated by Matt Freeman's accusing stare, he turned to the easy-smiling Ryan.

'Now, Ryan, my old trail buddy, I can see old sobersides Matt don't believe me. He reckons I'm drunk. But I'm as sober as a judge . . . two judges, goddamnit. Ain't that a fact, old pal?'

'Well, Kip,' Ryan said with a rueful smile, 'maybe not quite that sober. And we did need that mess of supplies kind of urgent, old son . . . '

'Sure, course you did. And I got 'em all loaded up in the buckboard out back by the livery right now . . . all ready to roll,' the waddy insisted, reassured by Ryan's amiable manner. 'So, why don't we have one for the road then get right on back to the herd, quick smart and pronto — what say?'

He reached for the bottle but Matt moved it out of reach. The cowboy stopped grinning, leather cheeks flushing hotly.

'What in hell!' he snarled, suddenly angry. 'Look, just on account you're the boss's son don't mean you got the right to — '

He broke off as Ryan's big hand clapped his shoulder. 'Take it easy, Kip,' he cautioned, strong fingers digging in hard to emphasise his words. 'No call for fussing, man.'

Cobb stared up into the tall man's face. He and Ryan Freeman had been good buddies on the trail. But he was uncomfortably conscious of the fact that the rancher's older son was real good with his fists, and outweighed him by a clear thirty pounds.

He seemed to sag a little then as he half-turned and slumped against the bar.

'It's that blasted trail!' he said with sudden emotion. 'That hot, stinking, back-breaking, lousy, dirty trail! Seems to me I been eating dust and prodding slab-faces all my goddamn life . . . and

6

finally I just had to bust out, I guess.'

It had grown quiet in the shadowy bar. Two nearby drinkers murmured desultorily. A chair creaked loudly when a card player twisted to drop a butt into a spittoon.

Cobb finally raised his sorry head to see what effect his words were having. Ryan grinned easily but Matt's face remained dark and cold.

'You don't have to put up with anything the rest of us don't, cowboy,' Matt stated flatly.

Cobb smashed a fist down on the bartop and drew his shoulders back. He was a strong man, hunked heavily in the shoulders with meat.

'Is that a fact, Freeman?' he snarled, giving in to booze and resentment now. 'Well, you are dead wrong, mister, on account what I've been putting up with — is you! I've ridden under a dozen trail bosses in my time but I ain't never rode under no sobersides slave-driver like you afore and that is the goddamn simple truth!'

By this everybody in the place was staring in the group's direction, and Matt's eyes blazed. He made to retort but his brother intervened.

'Now, Kip, you old sonova,' Ryan said soothingly, half-grinning, 'you've had one swallow too much firewater and that's a fact. How about you get on out to the buckboard and we head on back to the trail camp? Isn't that smarter than getting all hot and sweaty over nothing much at all?'

The cowboy hesitated, his sodden brain grappling with conflicting emotions and divided loyalties. He searched for a telling parting shot but it eluded him. He finally grabbed up his sweat-rimed sombrero, jammed it on to his head and weaved towards the batwings.

The louvred doors swung shut on the man's back and the clomp of boots faded into silence. Matt turned to his brother.

'Let's go,' he said tightly.

Ryan slung a muscular arm carelessly around his shoulders, teeth flashing in

8

his trademark smile.

'What's the hurry?' he queried. 'We rode fifteen miles to town after Cobb, no sense in sweating all the way back without at least a drink.'

For a moment Matt Freeman was ready to argue. He wished to return to the herd yet didn't want to quash his brother's enthusiasm. Reminding himself that he was sometimes critically referred to as 'the older brother' due to his seriousness in contrast to Ryan's exuberance, he shrugged, grinned and turned to the barkeep. 'Two big beers, Billy, and make it pronto!'

Each man was silent as he savoured the tingling pleasure of the cold beer.

Ryan Freeman was feeling good. He fervently believed a man could only go so long without a little hellraising. Besides, he wanted to get a few cold ones into Matt to help relax him some. His own easygoing ways were in sharp contrast to his brother's. Cobb was right in charging that Matt could be too tough on the crew at times. Ryan had seen no good reason to come down on the errant cowboy too hard, for he personally understood the many temptations inherent in a trip to town following a long stint on the trails.

Matt lowered his glass, waiting for the lift from the beer to hit, savouring the fine clean taste in his mouth. He studied his face in the bar mirror, idly noting the taut cheekbones and jet black thatch.

He looked part-Indian, he reflected, and couldn't help but be aware of the contrast between his dark image and his brother's blond handsomeness. Again he was mystified that two men of the same parents could be so different in appearance and nature.

As Ryan drained his glass he met his brother's glance in the mirror.

'Another?' he grinned.

'Why not? Hey, Billy!'

The hot afternoon died hard. The sun sunk towards the hills flinging long shadows across the streets of Wolflock. A storekeeper in white shirt and bombazine sleeve guards appeared on his porch to inhale the cool evening . . . cowboys rode in from the nearby spreads . . . from the back streets came the cries of children at play . . .

As the swift prairie darkness fell, lights began flickering on in the windows of the town. The noise from the Bird Cage increased steadily and spilled out into the street.

The now brightly-lit saloon was rapidly filling with thirsty punchers and grimed miners. Here and there stood lonely men with tied-down holsters. Who might this one be? A fugitive, drifter or maybe some lethal bounty hunter with wanted dodgers on his hip? No one knew, nobody asked. Any man's privacy was sacred in this bare-knuckled trail town.

Matt leaned lazily against the bar, a glass of rye whiskey in hand now. For the first time in long weeks he felt relaxed and free from the constant strain of the drive and realized just how badly he'd needed this break.

Beside him stood Ryan, straight and tall, his handsome face animated as he held a bunch of punchers enthralled with his recounting of a romance he'd once shared with a Mexican beauty who was encumbered by a husband of tremendous size and primitive temper.

Suddenly Ryan broke off as a slender dancing girl sauntered by, flipping her hips. He reached out and lightly touched her arm, bowing low when she turned towards him.

'Lovely lady,' he smiled, straightening to his full six-four. 'Would you do me and my brother the honour of sharing a glass with us?'

The girl, attractive in a faded kind of way, glanced nervously over one naked shoulder then back to the handsome cowboy.

'Well . . . ' she said doubtfully, obviously tempted.

'Sure you will, honey,' Ryan insisted. 'Clear the way now boys, make way for the little lady. This here feller is Mister Matt Freeman, and I'm Ryan.'

She nodded to Matt then turned back to Ryan. 'I am Lilly. I can really have only the one.'

'Sure, Miss Lilly, any little old thing you say.'

Matt grinned as he watched Ryan busy himself ordering more drinks while amusing the girl with his free-and-easy banter. His brother was in his element.

Moments later Matt suddenly realized the babble had dropped to a murmur in the saloon. The hands had moved away from the trio at the bar and he noticed one man dart an apprehensive glance towards the back table where the four black-jack players sat.

Though young in years Matt Freeman was mature in the ways of men and trouble. And it was trouble he suddenly detected hanging in the smoke-filled air of the Bird Cage Saloon.

Lowering his glass he studied the players. Two were hard-bitten rannies packing useful looking side-arms. The third man was massively built with a comically bovine expression. But it was the fourth player who captured and held the attention.

This one sat with his back to the wall, was tall and lithe-bodied and exhibited an animal-like grace of movement that was impressive.

Dressed mainly in dark garb, his face was commanding and saturnine under jet black hair which grew to a widow's peak on the forehead. Small black eyes appeared vaguely reptilian. Like his fellow players, this one was also watching Ryan and the dancing girl.

Matt turned enquiringly to a man standing nearby. The cowboy understood his look, and leaned over closer to whisper, 'Your friend is Cimarron Smith's girl.'

'Which one is Smith?' he asked.

'The hook-nosed joe in the red shirt. Best be wary, stranger. He's an owlhoot of some stripe with a rep as a gun-thrower.'

As the drinker moved off Matt studied Smith's tough red face and read danger there.

Quickly he assessed their situation.

They'd had a good day and it really was time to be heading back to the herd out on the plains. He saw nothing to be gained by maybe getting into a situation over dancing girl of brief acquaintance.

He tapped Ryan's shoulder. 'Let's ride, man.'

Ryan's eyes showed surprise. 'What for, amigo? Me and pretty Lilly are just getting acquainted, and the night is still young.'

'I figure maybe Lilly's got a prior engagement,' he said meaningfully to the girl, nodding towards the quartet in back. 'Isn't that so, Lilly?'

The girl followed his gaze and instantly sobered.

'Yes, your brother is right,' she said to Ryan. 'I . . . I really must go . . . good-bye . . .'

She was gone with a flick of crimson dress and a flash of silk stockings, darting up the staircase at the rear.

'What the hell . . . ?' Ryan said loudly, his testy temper flaring. He was turning to his brother when the ugly Smith rose jerkily from the card table and came lurching towards them.

Matt swore under his breath. He caught the whiff of real trouble. 'Let's go, man . . . ' he began but the red-faced little runt spoke over him.

'That's my woman you been messing with, saddle bum!' he flared. 'And just in case you got any big ideas, you better know I'm Cimarron Smith!'

Ryan had drunk quite a deal. His face flushed hotly.

'Is that a fact?' he retorted. 'Well, you're lucky you don't live back in Texas or you wouldn't have any woman to be worrying over. Why not? Well, back home we knock geezers as ugly as you on the head at birth.'

Matt groaned as the whole room fell silent. He knew they should have left sooner. The three men at the table were staring hard, and when Smith swung

16

his ugly head their way the man with the black eyes nodded reassuringly.

Cimarron Smith instantly puffed up and swung back on Ryan.

'You got a big mouth, cowboy. You want to back it up with something more than words?'

At that Matt stepped forward and grabbed Ryan by the elbow. He tried to shake him loose but Matt was both strong and determined.

'We're going — now!' he said and began hauling his brother towards the batwings.

'Hee hee!' Smith chortled derisively. 'They sure raise them big down in Texas, eh, boys? Big state, big ranches, and big yellow-bellies!'

His gaze swept the room, inviting the drinkers to appreciate his wit. Ryan had halted by this, and Matt realized Smith had to be silenced before the situation got out of hand.

Moving fast, he strode back to the man, who saw his clenched fists too late. A right hook caught Smith in the mid-section and the follow-up left to the jaw saw the man crash to the floor.

A sudden silence gripped the room.

Matt stepped back from the prone figure and swept the saloon with a warning look, his gaze lingering for a moment on the card-player in black who had not moved a muscle.

Then he turned quickly and was reaching for Ryan's elbow to drag him out by force, if need be.

But in that moment he saw his brother's face fill with sudden alarm.

'Watch out, Matt!' he shouted, then hurled Matt to one side with his left hand and grabbed his Colt with the right.

Twisting as he staggered, Matt had but a moment to take in the sight of a livid-faced Cimarron Smith, now up on one knee and face contorted with rage as the Colt in his hand swept upwards.

The roar of a shot was cannon-loud in the confined space and Smith was smashed backwards, dead before he hit the floor with a bullet in the heart.

A silence as deep as the grave embraced the Bird Cage Saloon. Violence was no stranger to this trail town — but then, neither was Cimarron Smith. In truth the man was a local hardcase hero, and Matt Freeman could feel the anger rising about them on all sides. Responding instantly to the danger, he backed up to his brother's side and palmed his .45 in one slick motion.

'All right, just stay put and keep your hands clear!' he ordered. 'That man drew first, and he aimed to back shoot. It was self-defence, pure and simple and you all know it. We're on our way, and if anyone makes to follow we'll — ' He broke off as the player in the black shirt rose from the table and came slowly towards them.

'Back off!' a pale-faced Ryan ordered. He cocked his revolver as the man kept coming. 'If you think we're kidding, take another step and you are dead meat — you'd better believe it.'

The man halted. Standing directly

beneath the central drop light he suddenly appeared taller and even more menacing.

'So — I believe you,' he said in a strangely soft voice that nonetheless hummed with menace. 'Now, you in turn can believe me.' He gestured. 'You just murdered a good man in cold blood. You might figure you'd get away with this, seeing as there is no law in a hundred miles, and hot-headed old Cim drawing first, and all. But the truth of it is, he was a pard of mine, so I'll be the judge and jury in this case. And I find you guilty,' he added, inclining his head at Ryan Freeman. 'And you'll pay for what you've done, I promise you that.'

The brothers traded glances. This whole scene was somehow unreal. Naturally they were shocked by the shooting but it had been inevitable and was a plain case of self-defence. They would already be gone on their way by this but for this stranger in black. They wanted to leave right now — yet his manner and what he'd just said seemed to hold them somehow.

Then Ryan made an impatient gesture and turned to go. 'You've said your piece,' he grated. 'It could be a big mistake to say any more, jasper.'

'Hold up!'

The man's voice was suddenly laced with authority. They turned to confront him again, Matt with a hint of reluctance but Ryan with arrogance and hostility showing plain.

'Do you know who I am?' they were asked.

'Reckon not, and I'm not exactly busting to find out,' Ryan snapped.

Red specks showed in the man's eyes. 'I'm Striker!'

Matt caught his breath. Striker! No man who rode the big trails was unfamiliar with that name. It was a name synonymous with the violence of a half-tamed land and conjured up a forbidding South-West gun legend.

But the older brother was not intimidated.

'And I'm Ryan Freeman, and this is my brother, Matt,' he stated, chin raised, smoking cutter still held firm in his grasp.

'Oh, I know . . . I know . . . ' For a long moment the man studied both from beneath hooked brows. Then he gave a wolfish smile. 'We'll surely meet again,' he said softly, then turning his back, made his way back to the table, stepping over the dead man indifferently.

The brothers traded glances then side by side walked out into the night.

The long ride back to the herd was uneventful and was made mostly in silence by Matt Freeman. By contrast, his brother talked incessantly and even laughed over the long day behind them, seeming to regard the gunplay and one more violent death as no more significant than some kind of dramatic play staged especially to entertain the brothers Freeman.

Matt was shocked yet understood Ryan was only being himself. His brother's world was big and self-assured, his own, by contrast, quiet and contained.

That was how they were shaped, men of the same blood, yet very different. And the strangest aspect of their shared lives as Eli Freeman's sons and heirs was their closeness despite, or perhaps because of, those very differences.

But Matt's thoughts grew heavier with the miles, nonetheless. He could still see Cimarron Smith's expression of disbelief the instant that single bullet smashed into him, how Ryan had faced the danger in the room without a hint of fear. But most vivid of all was the recollection of Striker's glitter-cold eyes, the man's whispery threat.

The night was growing chill about them and Matt turned up his shirt collar as they clop-hoofed past the wreckage of an ancient wagon half-buried in the red earth off the trail. He hunched his shoulders and began to hum some old Lone Star song. But it didn't help drown out that voice he was hearing again in the vast Texas night.

'We'll meet again!' the man named Striker had said. And with a strange sense of certainty, he knew they would.

2

The Revenger

The rain had come during the night and every rider had been in the saddle through the long miserable hours till dawn.

It was desperate work to keep a thousand head of cattle milling in a circle out on the rain-lashed plains, knowing that the next clap of thunder or jolt of chain lightning could trigger off a stampede.

Daylight brought an easing in the storm's violence but a chill rain still stung the riders who rode into camp, wolfed down beans and scalding coffee then remounted to go relieve the others still out with the herd.

Still brimming with characteristic energy despite a sleepless night, Ryan Freeman stood bareheaded in the rain giving the cowboys his embellished account of the shooting in Wolflock town, his brother standing unobserved beneath the canopy of the nearby chuck wagon, sipping at his coffee. Matt Freeman's face was sober as he listened to the the tale unfold, with Ryan firmly cast in the role of hero.

Matt suddenly stiffened as a rider sloshed past him to join his brother's group. It was Cobb, whom he'd sent into camp an hour earlier with instructions to return to the herd immediately.

Matt banged his mug down and crossed to the cowboy as he stepped down. He seized him by the shoulder and spun him around to face him.

'What's the idea, Cobb? I gave you an order and you didn't follow it. Well?'

Cobb's face flushed heatedly as he shook the hand away. 'You must think we're a bunch of goddamn slaves, Freeman,' he snarled. 'I only came in off nighthawk a short spell back, got handed a plate of beans and half a mug of cold coffee. I sure enough ain't mounting up again until I've at least had me a smoke and maybe a chance to breathe.'

From beneath his dripping hat brim, Matt studied the bigger man, tight-lipped. He was aware of the hush that had fallen over the others nearby, a silence that held until the only sounds were the pattering of the rain and the murmuring of the cattle.

'There's still lightning about and I need every man in the saddle,' Ryan said evenly. 'You've been missing the best part of an hour.'

'That's a lie, Freeman. Why don't you tell the truth for once? You've been looking for an excuse to fire me ever since we started out . . . and any lousy excuse will do. Now ain't that the truth?'

When Matt replied his voice was soft but his face was hard. 'That ties it! Fork up and draw your pay.'

Cobb's slab face reddened, sandy brows bristling as he made a violent gesture and loomed a threatening step closer.

'And just who elected you hirer and firer, mister? Your paw hired me back in Texas, and for your information he's the only one who can tell Kip Cobb he's through!'

'You're dead wrong about that, cowboy. Get your bedroll and go!'

Spinning on his heel Matt strode off for the remuda. Cobb, choking back a fierce oath came after him, big fists cocked. The sloshing of boots behind gave Freeman a brief warning. He swung around to parry a wild haymaker then sent the bigger man staggering with a blow to the ear that sent him crashing heavily into the flank of the wagon.

Enraged, Kip Cobb sprang back to confront him again at close quarters. 'All right, goddamn you! That does it brown. Put up your dukes and fight like a man, if you know how!'

'I'm not here to brawl, just to see a herd get through.'

For a moment Cobb stared angrily into Matt's dark face and cold eyes, torn between rage and common sense. Then with a curse he cocked his right fist ready to throw another punch when a tall figure suddenly stepped between them.

'Hold it, Cobb!' barked Ryan. He turned to his brother. 'What in tarnation is going on, Matt? Haven't we got enough on our plate without wrangling with the hired help? What in hell's this hooraw about anyway, man?'

Matt stood his ground stubbornly. 'I just fired him, is what. And this time he stays fired.'

'All on account I wanted to grab me a breather and maybe take a smoke before saddling again, Ryan,' Cobb protested. 'Damned if he ain't been trying to get shook of me ever since this drive started out!'

'Now, now, fellas,' Ryan drawled, raising both hands in a peaceful gesture. 'We've all had ourselves one hell of a tough drive and it ain't over yet, so let's not get to flying off the handle, huh? C'mon, what do you say?'

Ryan Freeman possessed a friendliness and natural charm. Every trail driver regarded him less as the boss's son than one of themselves, always ready to drink, fight or raise hell with the best of them.

The Ryan charm had worked often on the long drive, worked again now. And the rugged Cobb hung his head.

'Shucks, Ryan, I wasn't looking to ruckus, man. Just got a tad peeved, is all.'

'Sure you did — we all get that way times.' Ryan swung to face the others. 'OK, boys, how about it? Better get on back to the herd and let the other guys come in and grab a bite, huh?'

As one, the cowboys trouped for the remuda, swung into their saddles and headed out for the herd. Hands on hips, fair hair plastered flat from the rain, Ryan watched them vanish into the grey haze with a grin.

'Well, bro — ' he said turning, but let

the words hang in the air unfinished when he realized he was standing alone in the drizzling rain.

'Where is that crazy guy?' he muttered. Then, 'Hey, Charlie, where'd that brother of mine get to?'

Charlie Vance, cook for the drive, glanced up from his chores. 'Why, he grabbed Cobb's warbag out of the wagon and went stomping off over to your paw's tent. Wasn't looking any too happy neither, by the looks.'

Ryan sighed, clamped his sombrero on to his head and crossed to the far side of the camp where a slicker-draped tent stood surrounded by barrels, broken wheels and other accumulated essentials of a trail drive. The murmur of voices within ceased when he dragged the sodden flap aside and stepped inside.

He found Matt standing before their father Eli, grizzled and stern and seated upright at a camp table. His father's long time assistant and body-guard, quiet Jim Holloway, spoke low.

'Matt just told us he fired Cobb.'

Ryan spread his hands and grinned. 'Hell, Dad, we can't go around firing every rannie that shoots his big mouth off now and again. All the man wanted was to have a drag or two before he saddled up again. We've been riding the boys pretty hard of late and any geezer's liable to buck some when he gets pushed too far, I guess.'

'Cobb's caused a heap of trouble on this drive,' countered his father. 'Look what happened just yesterday on account of him.'

'Guess I'm not denying that,' Ryan replied. 'But Cobb's a big hard guy with plenty of oats in his brisket, and he and trouble have always had more than just a nodding acquaintance. But we can't afford to lose a top hand at this stage and I don't see that Matt had call to fire him.'

Eli Freeman tugged at his grey moustache and glanced from handsome Ryan to his younger son who was leaning against the tent pole, deft hands rolling a brown paper quirley.

'Well, Matt?' he grunted.

Matt cracked a match on his thumbnail, applied it to the weed and flicked out the tiny flame.

'You're in charge, Dad,' he said in his quiet way. 'I didn't fire Cobb just for what happened tonight but for the trouble he's caused a dozen times on the drive. He's got this rep as a big brawler and general tough guy, seems to feel he's got to live up to it. He has been itching to tangle with me ever since we quit Texas. A guy like that can foul up a whole drive, I've seen it happen.'

The rancher rose and drew back the flap to stare broodingly at the sodden landscape. Once again he found himself forced to make a decision where his sons disagreed. He suspected Matt's attitude towards the incident was possibly the right one, all things considered. But Matt was just the drive's scout and troubleshooter while Ryan was trail boss, and therefore was responsible for the discipline of the crew.

Then again, he mused, although his younger son could be stubborn at times, it was a fact of life that he was far and away the better worker, either back at the spread or on the drive. And this alone lent him added weight and status in his father's eyes.

With a sigh, he turned back to the men. 'Make up Cobb's pay, Jim.'

'But, Dad,' Ryan protested, 'we can't spare — '

Eli silenced him with a gesture.

'Matt fired him,' he reminded. 'He knows the men, good and bad, better than the rest of us. He saw fit to fire the man so he stays fired.'

Nobody spoke as Holloway methodically made up Cobb's wages and opened a steel cash box. He extracted a sheaf of green bills, counted them and slipped them into a brown envelope. He handed the package to Matt who took it in silence and moved to quit the tent.

His father halted him.

'One thing you likely don't know, boy. When I hired Cobb in Texas there was some talk he used to ride with some hardcases, maybe even outlaws. So . . . just be careful of him, hear?'

Matt gave his father a quizzical look which finally dissolved into a thin smile. 'Whatever you say, Dad.'

As he watched his son step out into the drizzle, Eli Freeman was reminded as he had often been during the drive that despite his youth Matt was always perfectly capable of handling any situation, and would doubtless do so again now.

Matt made his way to the remuda where his runty sorrel stood tethered. He removed his poncho from the saddle, slipped it over his shoulders then strapped Cobb's bedroll to the horse's back. In one lithe motion he was in the saddle and riding out towards the herd.

Once clear of the camp he pushed his cayuse hard down steep slopes of brush and out along a dark ridge line, dull red with scrub oak and berry bushes.

The climate was erratic for this time of year. Yesterday had been hot with the dust cloud from the big herd billowing for miles in the dry air. When the rain struck, the cold had come with it. From in back of him now a chill wind knifed out of the high country and sighed away amongst the trees with a sound like a woman weeping.

Soon he could make out the massive dark shape of the herd on the plains ahead, a cranky sodden army of humped backs, sweeping horns and drooping tails.

He cut across the churned wake of mud the cattle left in their wake, weaved through a sluggish scatter of stragglers, then fell in beside his top hand, Lance Haggert, who rode all hunched up in a streaming yellow mackinaw.

'They settled down?' he asked.

'I reckon,' the rider replied. 'No lightning about now and I guess we're over the worst of it.'

The man was about to speak again when he spotted the bedroll tied behind Freeman's saddle.

'Hey, ain't that Cobb's roll you got there?'

'That's right. And I've got his pay packet in my pocket. I want you to send a man up to replace him on point.'

Haggert stared blankly.

'Then you're really firing him?'

For a moment Matt didn't reply as he sat his mount gazing across the heaving sea of longhorns, blue eyes expressionless in his deeply tanned face.

'I sure as hell am,' he replied quietly, and heeled his mount into a canter.

Lance Haggert stared after him. Heedless of the rain, he tugged off his sombrero and scratched his thinning thatch vigorously.

'Whew! Young Matt just won't quit on anything once his mind is made up, and that's a fact. But he could have trouble with Cobb, though I guess he already knows that . . . '

Kip Cobb was not hard to find. Matt caught up with the man riding with Mailey out on the left flank. Both men leaned against the tormenting rain, a curl of tobacco smoke wisping out from beneath Cobb's hat brim. They turned at the sound of his horse.

Cobb eyed him sullenly, determined not to speak first. Then he sighted his warbag.

'What the hell are you doing with my stuff?' he demanded angrily.

Without reply, Freeman twisted and undid the straps holding the roll. Lifting it in both hands, he heaved it at Cobb, who was forced to catch it.

'What the hell . . . ?'

'You're through,' Matt said quietly.

The cowboy's notorious temper ignited. He heeled his mount close to Matt and grated his words out through yellowed teeth. 'You're all bluff and bulldust, Freeman. You don't have the guts to fire me, and we both know it.'

Matt slipped the envelope from inside his slicker and held it out.

'Here's your pay.'

To the watching Mailey, the seconds that followed were a bewildering blur of action. He saw Freeman proffer the package and Cobb slap it from his hand, sending the money spinning into the mud. But he barely saw the fist that lashed out to smack against Cobb's heavy jaw, sending the man spinning from his saddle.

Cobb lumbered to his feet, clothes dripping mud and his hat half-buried in the slush in back of him. The man was apoplectic with rage.

'All right, Freeman, you bastard. Daddy's big name and big money ain't going to stop you getting what you've had coming ever since this drive quit the ranch!'

Expressionless, Matt stepped down from his horse and stood awaiting the big man's charge, arms hanging loose, face blank.

The moment Cobb drew into range Matt swayed smoothly from his path and slammed a blow to the side of the head that had big Kip Cobb reeling sideways, arms flailing, surprised and hurt.

Yet he recovered fast to regain his balance. He sleeved his mouth, spat, and attacked again, slower and more wary this time.

The outcome was more of the same. Matt peppered his face with three lightning straight jabs then closed in and ripped a hook to the guts that had Kip Cobb buckling over his punching arm, his face a sudden sick grey.

'You . . . you goddamn upstart — ' the man managed to choke out in the split second before a brutal right hook smashed against his unprotected jaw and he hit the mud, face first.

He was half-drowning before Matt got his breath back then leaned down to turn him over. His face showed no expression as he said, 'Get up and get out. You are through!'

He signalled to Mailey as Cobb stumbled feebly to his feet, sobbing now in pain and humiliation.

'Get this bum on his horse!'

The hand obeyed with alacrity and Matt stood watching in wooden-faced silence as Cobb was boosted into his saddle. His roll was lashed on behind him and the pay packet tucked under the flap of his saddle-bag.

'Ride!' Matt ordered.

Mechanically, the man obeyed. Turning his horse away, he locked his shaking knees hard against the animal's flanks to avoid rolling off. Hoofs made a hollow sucking sound as he moved away in the rain.

Matt turned at the sound of hoofbeats to see a wide shouldered rider coming in fast. It was his brother, and he looked mad.

'Great day in the morning — what happened?' Ryan yelled, reining in alongside Cobb's horse.

No answer. With his jaw resting on his chest and eyes downcast, the defeated Cobb rode on leaving Ryan staring after him.

'I fired him,' Matt said.

Ryan glared at him for a long moment in silence. He then turned back to stare off after the hunched figure of maybe the toughest waddy on the drive. When he glanced across at Mailey, the man just shrugged. But it was an eloquent gesture that told Ryan most of what he needed to know.

'Reckon you did at that,' he said at length. 'You know, old Cobb was kind of a pard of mine and — '

'He stays fired!'

Ryan opened his mouth to retort but thought better of it. At the end of a minute's thick silence, he shrugged, grimaced then half-smiled. 'Come to think on it, old Cobb could be a pain in the rear end at times . . . I guess . . . '

Without response, Matt swung up and rode slowly off after the herd. Ryan leaned back against his mount and squinted at the distant speck that was his onetime drinking companion vanishing in the grey rain.

Cobb was no longer aware of the weather. As his head finally began to clear a steady stream of curses tumbled from battered lips. His head swam with plans for revenge which he discarded one after the other. For if nothing else, quiet Matt Freeman had proven himself the better man on the day, and Cobb didn't want to risk running into more of the same treatment, or at least not right now.

But that didn't mean it was over as far as Cobb was concerned. The man's whole stretch on the Freeman spread had been a sham and a fake from start to finish. He had signed on for the drive solely to evade the long arm of the law, with whom he was on the record as thief and badman.

It had worked while it lasted. Now he had grudges to settle and his former wild life that suited him far better to return to, should he choose.

Sure he wanted to get square with the Freemans. But more urgent than that, he wanted real excitement and big money excitement after six dreary months faking it as a cowboy just to avoid the foul clutches of the law.

'Now is the time to strike back at a few high-stepping sons of bitches and line your pockets with easy money, Kip old son. High time.'

But where to start — that was the question.

'Think, man, think!'

The name clicked into his head unexpectedly. Striker!

He reined in so sharply the horse grunted in protest. Cobb's beefy face was a study in concentration now. From all he'd heard of that shoot-out in Wolflock, that gunman Striker sounded like the real McCoy — the genuine article.

And surely that heller would have to be holding a big grudge against the Freemans over the killing of his pard.

Striker had made some big threats following the shooting — Ryan had told him so.

The man had a big score to settle.

He rolled and lighted a smoke with unsteady fingers, almost dizzy with his mounting excitement now.

'That Striker swore he'd get square — so he might only need the right kind of bait to convince him he oughta strike while the iron's still hot . . . '

He suddenly realized how it could all be done . . . big money to be made . . . Striker squares accounts with the Freemans . . . and, best of all, Kip Cobb gets rich and gets even all with the one roll of the dice . . .

He laughed aloud as he swung his horse south-west and booted it into a gallop. Two hours' riding would bring him to Wolflock.

3

Trail's End

Eli Freeman eased his position in the saddle as he watched the mass of trail-weary longhorns boiling about the catch gates leading to the chutes of the marshalling yards.

Freeman viewed the herd with mixed feelings. He had bred and raised every mean-eyed critter in the mob which numbered just a handful under one thousand head, and felt a twinge of genuine regret at the thought that by dawn they would all be on the St Louis freights to fulfil the needs of a meat-hungry East.

'Meanest critters God ever put breath into,' he muttered. 'But, damn it all, sometimes this part of a drive can be like losing kinfolk.'

An hour before, he'd sat down to talk

business with Jake Brills, the stock buyer. During the drive to Clantonville he had mentally rehearsed his meeting with that hardnosed dealer. He planned to threaten to swing the herd about and drive it back to Texas if he didn't get twenty-five dollars a head.

Then, if the man beat him down to twenty, he could accept it gladly and still be well ahead.

The dealer had personally accompanied him to the yards and had stood in silence, beady eyes playing over the restless mob. Later, in his large and airy office, the fat man had seemed lost in thought or maybe was on the verge of dropping off into a doze.

Then abruptly he snapped wide awake, drilled the rancher with eyes suddenly dagger sharp and slapped his desk top. 'Thirty dollars and not one cent more, you robbing old Texan bullwacker!'

Eli was stunned. 'Th-thirty bucks?'

'Now, don't you try and jack me up, Eli Freeman. I'm the biggest buyer in

47

Clantonville and I pay the best prices. No way known will I pay one cent more than thirty dollars a head — take it or leave it.'

The cattleman was dumbfounded. He'd been ready to accept twenty!

'Well, Jake, folks have always said you're the toughest there is in the business, and I guess they are right. So, I'll just have to take it, I guess. It's a deal.'

'Done!'

It was a fact of life that Eli Freeman was a stern and sober man of the land rarely given to impulsiveness, much less frivolity. Yet a mischievous twinkle in his eye was evident a short time later when he sighted the two horsemen approaching through the haze of marshalling yards dust.

'Sorry, boys,' he said in answer to their unasked question as they reined in. 'He wouldn't pay twenty.'

Matt cursed and his brother whipped off his trail-stained Stetson and flung its viciously to ground, yellow thatch glinting in the late afternoon sun.

'You settled for less?' he roared. 'We spend three solid weeks rounding up this bunch . . . we sign on fifteen cranky drovers to drive a thousand head of maverick, no-brain longhorns across two hundred miles of the roughest, hottest, dustiest and meanest cow-trail in the whole blue-eyed world . . . for what? For you to let a rattlesnake posing as a Yankee dealer gyp you for a price you should have rightly shot him for even suggesting! I . . . I . . . '

He couldn't go on. Spent by his outburst, Ryan slumped dramatically across his cayuse's neck, his gaze, dark and brooding now roaming morosely over what could be seen of the herd through the red veils of dust.

Matt moved his horse across to his father's side, lean face as usual almost expressionless despite the tension.

'Why didn't you do what we agreed on, Dad? If we didn't make the twenty we wouldn't sell. We all agreed on that, yet you — '

'And I didn't take twenty, did I?' the old man said with a rare twinkle. He looked from one to the other, dragging out the moment, savouring it. Suddenly he whipped off his hat and hurled it into the sky as he yelled, 'On account I sat back and let that thieving, bloodless son of a bitch pay us thirty!'

'Why you lying old — ' Ryan yelled, and heeling his horse across with a laugh, started in slapping Eli across the back with his hat while Matt just sat his saddle and smiled in huge relief.

'Thirty dollars!' he kept repeating. Then reached down and squeezed his father's arm. 'Never doubted you could do it, Dad, not really.'

'What are we going to do with all that dinero?' Ryan hollered. 'A thousand at thirty a head, why that's . . . that's . . . '

'It's a whole heap more than we'll end up getting if you two don't go give the boys a hand to yard them up before they rot away, and we end up just selling hides,' the rancher yelled. 'Go on, get!'

With the skill and grace of a Comanche, Ryan Freeman bent low and swept his hat off the ground then heeled his big mount towards the sea of beef, whooping and hollering at the top of his lungs.

Smiling broadly, Matt kicked his horse into a trot and followed.

Back in their dust, the rancher leaned his arms on the pommel and watched his sons expertly working the cattle, as only they could. His gaze grew reflective while he mused, as he did so often these days, on the strange fact that though both were of his own flesh and blood, they were as little alike as east and west.

Ryan had arrived first. Old Eli would never forget his Mary holding the squalling, red-faced bundle and saying softly, 'Our son, Eli.' Right from the beginning, Ryan had been a son to be proud of and brag about, quickly growing tall, broad of shoulder and undeniably handsome. Women flirted shamelessly with him while still a youth, men learned to respect and even fear him. The cowboys would ride clear to Doomsday for him if he wanted.

With his striking good looks and volatile temper, the elder son and trouble were natural partners.

Time and again his father would threaten to take a stockwhip to him, and Ryan, filled with genuine remorse, would turn his blue eyes on him and mutter, 'Sorry, Dad, just lost my head.' And likely as not they would then get boisterously drunk together on Eli's fine old brandy.

Matt's coming into the world had shadowed Eli Freeman's life. In giving birth to her second and last son, Mary Freeman died. It was a long time before Eli could take any interest in the boy, and for years had harboured a secret unworthy resentment against him for causing his wife's death.

Whereas Ryan favoured his father in appearance, Matt was lean and dark with a head of lustrous black hair, a heritage from Mary Freeman's mother, a full-blooded Mimbres Apache.

Instinctively it seemed, Matt had sensed his father's reserve towards him and by the time Eli had overcome his illogical resentment there was a wall between father and son which had never been completely broken down.

From a solitary, quiet boy, Matt grew into a lithe and powerful man, his Indian ancestry showing in his quick, supple walk and the black brows and broad cheekbones. Matt had never attracted people in the same way as did Ryan, but developed a strength of both body and mind that belied his calm manner. In his twenty-one years of life, Eli Freeman had never known his younger son not to finish an appointed task, nor concede victory to either man or beast.

In truth, it was Matt's unsmiling, implacable determination which often caused people about him to feel uneasy. Eli would never have admitted it but he himself was sometimes one of these.

Bright splashes of artificial light blazed from the Big Wheel, the Pair o' Dice and Fat Maisie's as the Freemans walked their horses slowly along the main street of Clantonville.

A dance-hall girl's husky song, backed up by a brassy, open-topped piano, drifted into the street:

'Where are the arms that held me,
Where are the lips I kissed?
Come to me, come to me, darling,
I'll show you how much you've been missed.'

The song stirred Ryan. How long had it been since he had danced or seriously flirted? Too damned long, was the right answer. He'd been weeks upon the endless trail with mean cows and cranky hands his only company. Not until trail's end had he found time for pleasure, and that had ended in disaster. Overall, there had been no time for fun. Just eat, sleep and ride, day after eternal day. But it was over at last and nobody was more excited than he.

For this was Clantonville, Kansas, and right within reaching distance were liquor, cards, excitement — and girls. Plus the time and money to make the most of them all, either singly or all at once, made never no mind to this long rider.

Or so he hoped. His high-flying plans had not exactly been cleared, as yet.

He ran a tongue tip over dry lips and cleared his throat noisily.

'Er, Dad, reckon we'll overnight here and take the boys' wages out to the camp in the morning, huh?'

'We sure enough will do no such thing. Those men have worked every bit as hard as ourselves and they have just as much right to a big blow-out as I know you two are looking for. No, we'll go to the hotel, wash up and shave first. Then we will have us a meal and go on to pick up the cash from Brills, and you and your brother can take their pay out to the hands tonight.'

Ryan's eyes showed his disappointment and anger. 'Damn it all to hell, old man! We're bushed. All I'm fit for tonight is to spread out on a big feather bed and sleep until — '

'You don't fool me any, you young whelp,' Freeman chuckled. 'You're just itching to cut loose amongst the red-eye and dancing girls, and I know it. Well, you're just going to have to wait till tomorrow. That won't kill you.'

'Might as bloody well!'

They rode on to the Stockman Hotel. Immediately, Ryan flung himself from his saddle, hitched his horse and stomped bad-temperedly across the porch and disappeared inside.

Smiling at the tantrum, Matt and Eli followed.

The Stockman had been built in the earliest days of Clantonville. It had been, and still was, the town's finest structure. Built by its owner as a replica of the Great Eastern in Savannah, it towered three floors high with an upper balcony commanding a view of town and countryside. True to its model it featured huge, drape-hung windows and was lit up tonight like the Fourth of July.

The cattle king did not stay here for show. He simply liked comfort and this time around could afford to pay for it.

A sniffy clerk glanced up in alarm as three trail-grimed men, rowel spurs jingling, tramped across the expensive carpet to his desk.

'Can I assist?' he asked coldly. 'You are looking for the tradesmen's, perhaps?'

Reacting, Eli Freeman fixed him with a stare that could cower a barnacled cowhand at thirty paces.

'My name is Freeman. Eli Freeman. I have a booking for three rooms with baths.' He carelessly flung a large bill on to the desktop. 'Let me know when that cuts out and I might pay up, or I could easily sue you for overcharging!'

It was a treat to trail-strained eyes to see the clerk buckle and obsequiously invite the guests to sign the register

57

— 'If you would be so kind, gentlemen?'

Father and son enjoyed the whole thing. Not so brother Ryan who, still riled, stood aloof across the foyer, towering over everyone in sight.

Ryan turned his head loftily to sight a young woman eying him with frank interest. She was slim, full-breasted and attractive.

When he arched a laconic eyebrow the girl gave a faint quirk of the lips then turned away.

'Hey, Ryan!'

He turned his head to see Matt and his father beckoning.

'Come on, stop sulking, damnit!' Eli called. 'We've got plenty to do tonight, so stir your stumps.'

When Eli Freeman issued orders you paid attention.

With a sigh and a scowl, Ryan put his pride in his pocket and crossed the lobby to rejoin them.

As the three made for the stairs, Ryan turned for one last look — and there she was — eying him off again. Suddenly stimulated and his tantrum passed, his back snapped straight and he danced up the staircase with an athletic step, thinking now: 'Tomorrow I'll really take this hick town apart and make them remember it — yessir!'

It took an hour to remove stubborn whiskers, bathe away weeks of sweat and trail dust and climb gratefully into fresh rig.

Upon entering the chandeliered dining-room they now blended comfortably with the well-dressed diners, apart from the six-gun each Texan wore at his hip.

A hearty meal completed, they quit the hotel and strolled along the sidewalk. They were chatting amiably when, coming towards them, they saw a stranger sporting twin six-shooters buckled low around slender hips.

The man glanced sharply at them, and the brothers tensed a little, then turned their heads to watch him pass on by.

The brothers' eyes locked. Wolflock was well behind them and the shooting incident hadn't even made the papers here. It was a raw and violent land and just another saloon shoot-out was scarcely news. Yet it had been a major event for them which for some reason was proving difficult to put behind them, and both were still wary and on edge as a consequence.

They didn't discuss it yet each knew the reason for this. It was not the shoot-out that they recalled so much as the man who had confronted them in its immediate aftermath.

The one called Striker.

There had been something deeply sinister about that *hombre* that somehow stayed with a man.

'So, why's everybody gone quiet on me of a sudden?' Eli demanded suspiciously.

'Huh?' Ryan said, winking at his brother. 'Hell, we're not quiet, old man. We're just so used to you jawboning like an old fishwife all the time I guess we thought you were still babbling on.'

Eli actually chuckled, and Matt wished he could be that free-and-easy with him, while knowing it could never be that way.

Leading the way at a brisk pace Eli eventually brought them to a halt before a small, white-painted brick office with a canvas awning. The words, 'Jacob Brills, Stockbuyer and Dealer' were inscribed in bold black letters upon the window.

In response to their knock a pot-bellied man chewing an unlighted cigar opened the door holding a Remington .32 rifle in brawny hands.

'Let them in, Cable,' a voice growled. 'It's the Freemans. Er . . . excuse the gun, Eli, but I carry quite a bit of cash here and I take no chances.'

They entered the cluttered office.

'You've met my boys, Matt and Ryan?' Eli said. The beefy man rising from his padded chair nodded, and he went on. 'Have you got the payroll made up for me like I ordered?'

'Sure have. It's all right here if you want to check it out. One thousand two-fifty dollars in bills and coin in fifteen individual bags, with each rider's name on the tag.'

Freeman spent several minutes checking out the bags at random until satisfied everything was in order.

'Good work, Jacob. All right boys, pack these away in the satchel and get straight out to the camp. Those poor, thirst-crazed drover boys will be fearing we'll never show up by about now.'

Brills looked on as the brothers quickly filled the big black satchel. He frowned. 'Don't you reckon you boys might be taking a risk, just the two of you escorting a sizeable passel of money like that . . . then carting it to hell and gone out on to the prairie at night? Better take Cable with you. He really knows how to handle that rifle of his.'

Matt finished buckling the satchel straps, and straightened. 'Nothing to worry about, Mr Brills. After nursing a thousand head of half-wild beef across three territories, this here looks like boys' work. Right, Dad?'

'These men know what they are doing, Jake,' Eli affirmed proudly. 'Just twixt you and me, I reckon any low thief who worked up the grit to tangle with a pair of half-wild Texicans like these two, would pretty soon be wishing he'd taken on the entire Comanche Nation instead.'

Praise from Eli Freeman was about as rare as saloons in Death Valley, and the sons beamed smugly. But the father quickly brought them back to reality.

'You know, if you two are intending to stand there smirking and preening all night, pretty soon we'll have a whole trail crew stampeding in here looking for us and their drive pay. So, vamoose!'

'That's our pappy,' Luke grinned at the dealer. 'A sweet and lovable old Southern gentleman.'

He swung to Matt, turning serious. 'C'mon, man, if we stir our stumps we can be out in an hour, finish paying them off by ten-thirty, be back here by half-eleven. Things should be just warming up by then, so let's hustle!'

The pear-shaped Cable got the door and the two strode from the office, the satchel swinging between them. The sounds of their footsteps were quickly swallowed by the night.

Brills opened a box of expensive cigars and for some time he and the rancher discussed topics close to the hearts of cattlemen the west over. Finally Freeman rose and stretched.

'Guess I'll be heading back to the hotel and that big comfortable-looking bed. It's times like this a man realizes he's not a yearling any longer.'

'Ahh, by the look of you there's a lot more drives left in you yet, Freeman,' the dealer said, rising. Then with a frown he bent and picked up a slip of printed paper from the floor. 'Goldurn, look at this!'

'What?'

'It's the master payslip. They must have dropped it without knowing. They won't be able to pay your men without it. Cable, you'd better take this and go see if you can't catch them up.'

'Never mind, Cable, I'll take it,' said the rancher. 'I know where their horses are liveried, and they won't have time to have them saddled up and ready by the time I catch up.'

He started for the door. 'See you in the morning, Jake, got to move sharp.'

Eli Freeman moved briskly along the plankwalk, weaving his way through miners, cowboys and pretty women all en route from one watering hole to another. He passed the noisy Pair O' Dice and cut down a long and gloomy alley, taking the short cut to the corral in back of the Stockman Hotel.

He was nearing the end of the alley when he paused as something stirred in the darkness close by.

'Who is it?' he called, hand on gunbutt.

A soft moan came from the shadows. Stepping closer, he made out the dim form of a man lying face-downwards in the litter and dust. Instantly he dropped to one knee.

'What's up, partner? What's ailing you?' He turned the man on his back. 'OK, now what is going — Ryan!'

Slowly, painfully, the tall figure opened his eyes. By the faint light Eli could make out the dark bloodstain running from hairline to jaw.

'Ryan! What in tarnation happened, boy? Where . . . where is your brother?'

'Somewhere . . . somewhere close by . . . ' Ryan Freeman sounded like a man trying to speak underwater.

Eyes stabbing the darkness, the rancher suddenly spied the second him shape nearby, lying ominously still. Heart thudding with apprehension, he bent low and stared at the pale face. Matt's face was also bloodied and one eye was badly discoloured, his forehead deeply gashed down one side.

'Boy . . . boy!' he gasped, swabbing at the blood with his kerchief. Then he felt the faint whiff of breath stir his grey moustache and groaned, 'Thank God!'

'Dad!'

Responding to Ryan's strengthening voice, he gently lowered Matt's head to the ground and returned to the older brother's side. Ryan had managed to prop himself upon one elbow and lay shaking his head to clear it, a banner of yellow hair tumbling across his face.

'What in hell happened, boy?'

'We . . . we were jumped. Three . . . maybe four hellions, I calculate. They were waiting for us . . . must have known we'd left the livery by this alley and would likely come back the same way. Hell! Matt and I were double watchful and careful — but these robbers were good, I'll give them that. One second they appeared, the next we were going down like nine pins. I . . . I can't see the satchel. Sorry, Dad . . . '

Exhausted by his effort, Ryan sagged, resting his head upon his arm. His wound was still bleeding as he slumped in the dust.

Fury glittered in Eli Freeman's eyes. He sprang erect and now his .45 filled his hand. 'Stinking dirty dry-gulchers! Half-killing my boys and stealing the payroll . . . Can't have had time to get far — ' He broke off. The sudden rumble of hoofs from the box street close by galvanized him into instant action. Cocking his Colt, jaw set like a rock, he leapt Ryan's body and sprang for the alley mouth with the vigour of a young and angry man.

As he reached the street a quartet of dark horsemen came storming his way from the dead-end, coat-tails flapping, sparks flying from steel-shod hoofs.

In the ghostly moonlight he clearly made out the shape of the satchel swinging from the lead rider's saddle horn.

His Colt glinted as he swung it up.

Gunflame erupted from a horseman's dark bulk in an orange-red ball and a slug smashed into the wall above the rancher's head. Instantly his .45 responded. A jagged scream was torn from the rider's throat as the heavy slug caught him squarely in the chest, hammering him backwards out of the saddle to bounce over the horse's rump and crash into the road.

The corpse was still rolling as the lead rider suddenly broke away from the bunch, turned and drove his mount directly back towards the cattle-man's crouched figure.

It was the last thing Freeman expected. It threw him for a moment ... and that proved to be his last moment this side of eternity ...

Flame belched from the cattleman's Colt. But he fired too quickly and the looming bulk of the rushing horse and rider affected his aim. Suddenly the tall rider was directly above him, and he saw his face with vivid clarity — dark, glitter-eyed and cruel with lips skinned back in a savage grimace.

Eli Freeman attempted to fire again but by this the leaning horseman's revolver was almost touching his face before a fierce and brilliant burst of flame seemed to engulf the world.

As the killer whirled and stormed

away in the wake of his henchmen, the cattleman swayed, both hands clamped to his head where the .45 slug had smashed into the brain. It was a dead man who tottered two faltering steps before crashing on his back, the already glazing eyes staring up at the Kansas moon.

4

Watch His Face!

Kip Cobb was dying.

Sprawled upon a blanket-covered table in the town marshal's office, his breath coming in long, painful gasps, he could feel the shadows drawing in.

Eli Freeman's bullet had struck the man squarely in the chest, piercing his lungs. The fall from the fast-running horse had smashed his spine. The man's body was no longer the power-house machine it had always been. His life had shrunken down to a throbbing landscape of agony from which there could be no relief.

'Tell us who was with you, Cobb!'

Weakly, Cobb rolled his head to the side and stared into the gaunt, bearded face of Marshal Vager. At the lawman's side stood two of his deputies, while leaning wearily against the rolltop desk was Doc Mallon.

A fresh wave of agony clutched the outlaw; his eyes screwed tight and crimson dribbled from the corner of his mouth.

The marshal lent over the table. 'You owe them no loyalty, man. They rode off leaving you to die like a dog. That's the breed of pards they were. Just tell me one thing. Who was the tall man, the one in the black rig?'

The heller opened his eyes. The grimed plaster ceiling appeared to be an impossible height above him. 'Dirty, Judas bastards . . . I'd . . . I'd have stopped for them . . . seen them through . . .'

His eyes closed again.

Doc Mallon stirred himself and lifted the dying man's wrist with pale, delicate fingers. 'He's mighty close to it, Marshal; maybe five minutes left, could be less.'

'Cobb, your number is up so do one decent thing before you go,' the marshal said urgently. 'Just say who was the man in black.'

The wild man's eyes were shut tightly against the pain yet his voice was clear. Every man in the stuffy room heard his final word.

'Striker!'

Marshal Vager emitted a long sigh of relief as he straightened. He turned to the medico.

'Stay with him, Doc. Do whatever you can to make it easier for him.' And, picking up his hat, he walked from the room.

Clantonville was quiet all about him as the lawman trod the narrow plankwalk.

His path led directly by Hanlon's grim mortuary where the shutters were closed with tiny shafts of light showing here and there. Inside, Hobe Hanlon was busily working on Eli Freeman's body, fixing it up some so that tomorrow friends and riders could come pay their last respects.

Vager had been a lawman all his life.

He had seen numberless killings, witnessed an Indian massacre in Colorado, had fought it out on many an owlhoot trail in his time. Yet tonight's killing had hit him brutally hard.

He had known the rancher for almost as long as he could remember. They had never been close friends; the lawman was not the kind who made friends, yet a deep respect had existed between the formidable cattle king and the solitary marshal. It just didn't seem fitting for a fine old man to have gone this way. Had Vager ever allowed his imagination to wander that far, he might have pictured Freeman one day dying peacefully in his bed surrounded by his boys and loyal riders. Instead he'd died far from home, gunned down in a back alley by some dirty outlaw.

As the lawman mounted the steps of the Pair o' Dice, the knot of men gathered there made way.

They looked at him expectantly. Stony-faced, he moved on past them and shouldered his way through the doors.

The place was crowded but there was little noise, no gaiety. Men sat in low-murmuring groups at the tables, smoking and talking and nursing their drinks.

Every so often someone might glance across at the round table by the staircase where Ryan and Matt Freeman sat with Lance Haggert, trail boss of the herd.

The marshal made his sombre way across to the group, drew out a chair and lowered his lean body into it.

Total silence descended upon the room as a pale Ryan Freeman stared at the marshal.

'Cobb dead yet?'

'By now, I'd say yes,' replied Vager.

A pause of some seconds. Then, 'Did he talk?'

Clantonville's peace officer looked in turn at the three faces that were intently scrutinizing his own. Slowly and deliberately he reached for a whiskey bottle and poured himself a double.

'He talked.'

He spoke loudly, his voice carried. A murmur swept through the place and chairs scraped loudly as drinkers clambered to their feet and closed in on the round table. Matt Freeman leaned forward in his chair, his face set like a stone. His brother remained unmoving, rock-still with his ice-blue eyes riveted on the lawman as he tossed his head back to swallow his double at a gulp.

'Yeah, he talked right enough.' He paused for a moment. 'It was Striker.'

An angry murmur rose to a roar from a hundred throats. Ryan Freeman finally leaned back in his chair, an expression of grim satisfaction working his features. His brother's face, by contrast, remained a blank mask.

It was Lance Haggert who spoke first. 'But I always had Striker figured out as gunfighter — you know? A real pro, sure, but not a back-alley killer.'

'You're dead wrong, son,' sighed the

peace officer. 'Striker would kill any-body, anytime, anyhow. He's wanted in three states and four territories, but up until now I haven't been able to touch him here legally. He's killed here, sure. But it's always been after goading some poor sucker into going for iron first, then cutting him down like a dog with, I guess, about the fastest hand there is.'

It fell silent again as they absorbed that statement. Then one of the cowhands jumped to his feet and bawled; 'Well, what are we all setting about jawing for? Let's get us a posse together, run the varmint down and swing him off the tallest tree in Kansas!'

The mob roared in agreement. Cries of 'Lynch him! . . . No good killer!' and 'Somebody go get a good rope!' rose from all sides.

Marshal Vager rose and held up a silencing hand.

The shouting ceased.

'Before we all go off half-cocked, boys. This here Striker and his dirty butchering bunch have got a long head start and at the rate they left town they could be ten-twenty miles away by now. It's getting on towards moonset and we wouldn't pick up their sign in the dark.'

'Wal, we'll get everything ready and ride out at first light!' a bearded miner shouted.

Again cries of assent, but once more the lawman motioned for silence. When he spoke now his tone was low and reasoning.

'Boys, I only know so much about this Striker. But I do know records show he started out riding the owlhoot at about twelve, thirteen. He can stay alive on the smell of an oily rag and he can hide his mean frame in a pickle barrel. Once, he got holed up by a posse of forty armed men after he shot a woman in Sante Fe. Jokers who knew that blind canyon said it wasn't possible to get out. Well, they closed in and Striker was gone. They never did find out how he did it, but he sure enough did.'

'Well, git to the point, Marshal,' a

78

man growled. 'What are you trying to say?'

'Yeah, Marshal,' supported Haggert. 'We ain't following you all that clear.'

The lawman hooked thumbs in shellbelt and spoke quietly.

'I'll make it quick and simple, Haggert. Striker won't be caught in a day nor a week. His bunch is travelling fast and it's travelling light. If I was to form a posse of say, a dozen riders, how much do you figure we'd have to pack? And how many men have got the time to spend maybe a month hunting down a bunch of owlhoots? It doesn't take a heap of figuring that a posse just plain ain't practical.'

Ryan rose and moved around to face the lawman, feet planted wide. His wound had been cleansed and dressed, and apart from a slight paleness he was showing little effect of the gun whipping.

'I reckon you're right, Marshal. A posse of men wouldn't have much hope of catching up with a pro like Striker.

But that sure doesn't mean he'll get away. There'll be two men riding out of this town in the morning on two of the best horses in Kansas, and they won't be stopping riding until Striker has stopped breathing. You can wager good money on that.'

He inclined his head towards his brother. 'Isn't that so, Matt?' he demanded, and Matt Freeman nodded.

Vager reached out and grabbed Ryan's shoulder.

'Now, just a minute, boy. That isn't the way to go about a thing like this. We lost a good man tonight and we can't afford to lose two more.' He gripped harder. 'Let the law handle it, son. Striker's gone too far this time, he'll hang soon enough.'

Ryan shook the hand away. His voice was harsh when he spoke.

'You're plain wasting your time, Vager. I'm begrudging that killer every breath he takes from here on in. But I'll guarantee he won't be taking many more. Matt and me have come up against scum aplenty in our time and we're still alive to tell about it, so don't waste any advice on us. You can give it to Striker should you chance to cross his trail, for he's sure the one who's going to need it.'

He turned his broad back on the peace officer, shoved a chair aside and crossed to the bar.

Suddenly the lawman looked very old and tired. He turned slowly to look hopefully at Matt. But the dark young cowboy's expression was wooden, his eyes cold.

Without another word, the lawman collected his hat, mechanically put it on and walked from the saloon.

As the batwings flapped shut, a young rider moved across to the bar at Ryan's side. He was a slender, pock-marked youth named Ruby who had a wide reputation as a dab hand with a .45.

He said, 'Ryan, at least let me come along with you. Your paw was real good to me and I'd sure like to help run his killer down.' He patted his gun handle significantly. 'I reckon you'd find me real handy to have along.'

Ryan turned to Ruby and the room, his face cold, composed and determined.

He said, 'Thanks, Ruby, but I do believe me and Matt can take care of it.' Then to the others, 'I know how you all feel and I'm proud of you. I'd admire to have you ride along with us but I wouldn't want to see any man risk his neck. Just remember this: when I swing Striker, I'll be doing it for all of you as much as for my brother and me.'

It ended there.

★   ★   ★

The hours dragged by and, but for the Pair o' Dice, Clantonville lay in darkness. The night sky was thickly sown with a million stars. Somewhere far out on the prairie, a kit fox barked sharply, a cottontail scuttled away in alarm, and the night was still again.

In the shadows of the saloon porch,

Matt Freeman leaned against a stanchion, twisting a cigarette into shape. A vesta flared briefly in his hand, illuminating the dark, strong-boned face, the bandage on his forehead showing out starkly white.

The pain inside was easing at last.

Father and brother were the only folks he'd ever known, and now Eli was gone. Secretly in his heart, Matt was aware that he'd always been closer to his father than he had ever been to his brother, yet he wondered if Eli had ever known the true strength of his feelings for him.

Probably not, he reflected. And now it was too late.

He had always envied his brother's easy manner and boundless self-confidence. He recalled Ryan's habit of creeping up behind Eli and seizing him in a crushing wrestler's grip, and then the two would engage in a wild rough and tumble, roaring curses and affectionate insults until collapsing, laughing and spent.

The memories were sharper than ever tonight, as was the guilt he'd experienced because of his twinges of jealousy at such times. Why couldn't he have been more like that with the old man? Well, too late now.

He turned and looked through the saloon window where Ryan was visible standing at the bar, towering over the men surrounding him. They were assisting him plan out his campaign to catch the killer, some offering unnecessary advice on what to do with him when caught.

Ryan was halfway over Eli's death already, he could tell. The wild grief was behind him and his features were now animated, his mind humming with plans for retribution.

Matt turned back to the street, envious of the other's strength and resilience in a crisis. Did Ryan feel any guilt over the affair? Probably not, although he certainly did. He was convinced in his own mind that he'd been at least indirectly responsible for the bloody events of the day. For it was he who had wounded Striker in Wolflock and set the killer on their trail. It was also he who had fired at, then whipped Kip Cobb. Searching his conscience, however, he still could not see how either incident might have been avoided.

He believed now he could accurately guess what had occurred following his encounter with both men. Striker had crossed trails with Cobb. Cobb knew about the big payoff due at drive's end in Clantonville, and Striker had seen the opportunity both to even accounts with them and pick up a swag of dollars at the same time. Now his father was dead as a result.

He glanced up at a soft footfall.

'Hi, Jim,' he said.

The small, buckskin-garbed man stood in the square of light spilling from the saloon window.

'Guess there's no call for me to say how I feel about your dad, Matt,' Holloway said in the soft and southern-burred voice he knew so well.

'Thanks, Jim,' Matt replied. 'I always figured Pa meant about the same to you as he did to me and Ryan.'

The two stood in silence for a spell. Matt flicked his cigarette away, watching it curve through the air like a falling star. It hissed briefly on landing in a puddle in the middle of the street. Dead.

He turned a little in order to study his smaller companion who was gazing unseeingly at the saloon window.

Jim Holloway was a neat, quiet man who wore his buckskins like a broadcloth suit. His rig was always clean, and fitted perfectly. His face never showed a bristle. Even on the dust-choked trails he always managed to give the impression he could be just returning from an evening in town. Matt smiled as he saw him carefully adjust the knotted silk bandanna he wore at his throat.

He studied the face. It was liberally scarred, eye-patched and unintentionally menacing due to the various distorting injuries it had suffered in the far past.

The single eye was black and unblinking.

This man had come to the Circle Bar twenty years back in a strange way. An outrider spotted dust rising and upon investigation came across a wild-eyed horse dragging what appeared to be a small dead man by a stirrup iron.

The man was not dead but did pack three bullets in his body. Miraculously he survived and had been Eli Freeman's right-hand-man from that day on.

Vague rumour subsequently painted Jim Holloway as a killer from the Mesquite Badlands. But Eli Freeman never questioned him about his past and no other man dared. He wore a silver-mounted Colt .45 on his right hip but had never been known to use it, such was the power and authority of his presence.

Jim Holloway was Matt Freeman's closest friend. These two quiet, iron-willed men were cut from the same cloth.

The older man cleared his throat.

'You're going after Striker.' It was more a statement of fact than a question.

'Yep.'

'Only fitting, I guess.' Holloway began building a cigarette with deft, sure fingers. 'I saw Striker in a gunfight two years back in Utah when I was there on business for your dad.' He blew a thin gust of tobacco smoke into the air. 'He is fast. Matter of fact you could call him quick as sudden death.'

Silence again. It seemed the little gunman had said all he needed to say. But then he turned to Matt and uncharacteristically clamped a strong hand to his shoulder. 'About two seconds before he drew and blew that geezer out of his boots, I noticed Striker seemed to lag deliberately a little, like he was purposely tempting fate. But then he hauled iron quicker than you could believe and it was all over. Could be a habit, then again it mightn't mean a damn thing. But, if you ever get to face him . . .'

He left the sentence unfinished. Matt

smiled and shook his hand. 'Obliged, Jim. Guess you know we'll be leaving you in charge? Now I'd best go get Ryan and see about getting started.'

Holloway watched him shoulder through the batwing doors, then, cigarette dangling from his lip he turned away and set off along the shadowy street.

He halted before the mortuary.

He remained outside the flat-roofed building for a long time like a small, compact statue, straight-backed and sombre as always, just staring always at the now darkened windows. From the unblinking black eye, a single tear fell.

★   ★   ★

When the first rays of the summer sun burst across the frowning Silver Lode Mountains the following morning, Ryan and Matt Freeman were already riding swiftly many miles from Clantonville following the killer's trail into the parched and dangerous South-West.

5

On The Dodge

Striker's supple hands caressed his gleaming Frontiersman model Colt .45 like a man stroking the hair of a beautiful woman, lovingly, almost reverently.

He held it up and watched the firelight sheen from its dull, blued surface. Then he spun it by the trigger guard, allowing the butt to slap smoothly into his palm. He held it close to his lips and blew a speck of dust from the sight.

'Do you have to play with that gol-durned piece like a baby with a rattle?' demanded the big, ox-shouldered figure seated across the fire.

Striker gave no sign he had heard. He produced a bandanna and commenced polishing the weapon, slowly and with complete concentration.

A minute passed.

Without glancing up from his chore, he asked very quietly, 'It bothers you some, does it, Big Boy?'

Magee couldn't read Striker's tone. He shifted his weight uneasily on the mossy boulder supporting his bulk.

'Well, no, guess it don't exactly bother me, boss, just rubs on my nerves some, if you know what I mean?'

Again a long silence as the killer continued to tinker with his deadly plaything.

'Reckon I don't, Big Boy. Just what do you mean?'

Magee's beefy face flushed, he stammered now. 'Gee, I never meant nothing . . . it's just that . . . well, you horsing around with that piece kind of . . . '

His words dried up and he turned an appealing glance on the third member of the bunch.

'What he means, Striker,' said Slinger Lee, 'is that whenever you see a man playing around with a shooter it just naturally makes you edgy. We've all seen guns go off by accident, and who wants to go that way? I always say an accidental shot can kill you just as dead as one that's meant to bore you.'

Striker's eyes never left the gun. With his fore-finger he spun the chamber several times listening to the rhythmic click of the well-oiled mechanism.

He rose lazily and with practised ease twirled the gun in the air, dropping it neatly into the tied-down holster.

He stood there, long and lean, the glow from the dogwood fire flickering across his face.

'Well, if you boys don't beat all,' he drawled. 'When we agreed to pard-up I thought you were middling tough *hombres* with grit in your guts who could back my play. But where do I find myself? Stranded way out on the lonesome prairie with a pair of big, bad outlaws who get jittery at the sight of a gun out of its leather. I declare that ties all!'

His voice was soft with the slurred vowel sounds of the South-West. Soft and menacing.

'Doggone it, boss,' protested Big Boy, tugging nervously at his earlobe. 'You was just making me jittery some, is all.'

'So you said before,' said Striker.

Slinger Lee moved from where he had been standing against a cotton-wood and crossed to the fire to face Striker squarely.

'Don't ride Big Boy, Striker. He doesn't rightly know how to take it. Ain't no call for it anyways.'

His voice was quiet.

Red lights glinted in Striker's eyes. He was a man of murderous rages and touchy vanity. For a handful of seconds he teetered on the edge of doing something he would surely regret — maybe even something that might see him killed. For Slinger Lee was marvellously quick with a Colt .45, maybe near as good as himself. Maybe . . .

He finally turned his back on the

man and held his hands out to the fire.

'You guys are jumpy and I know why,' he said. 'You saw a man blown away and you're scared a posse'll come loping along any minute and swing us high. Ain't that right?'

'Well, guess we got a right,' defended Magee. 'After what happened in Clantonville there's bound to be a chase after us.'

Striker sneered, 'Main thing I recall about that noplace town is that we collected thousands of bucks for five minutes' work.'

'What about that old varmint you shot? Old Freeman. If that don't stir up a whole mess of trouble then I don't know what would.'

'One detail you're disremembering, Big Boy, is that if I didn't drill that old buzzard when I did, his next slug might've got you. You'd be hard to miss, I reckon . . . and you saw what happened to Kip Cobb.'

'Damnit, what's all this wrangling about?' Lee was testy. 'We did a job, it paid off and now all we got to do is git as far from Kansas as we can, just as quick as we can. Simple enough, ain't it?'

Striker glared contemptuously over his shoulder at Big Boy, then shifted his gaze back to Lee.

'Guess I never could stand seeing a man start to crack up before my eyes, is all. Matter of fact, it turns my guts.'

Lee's face was ominously calm in the flickering light. 'Me and Big Boy go way back, Striker. We've pulled our big jobs and have been up and we've been down. But we always stick. We agreed to pard up with you and we like how you operate. But you mouthing off at him — and playing with that fool gun — that don't set well with me, if you get my drift?'

Seconds stalked the big plains silence. The fire popped and crackled and again uncertainty tainted the air.

But not for long. Abruptly Striker's hawk face split into a wide smile and he folded his arms to show he had no violent intentions.

For the stark truth of the matter was, he genuinely needed these two. He'd been holing up in a cow town when Lee and Magee had shown up, showing signs of tough times and hard riding. Plainly with much in common, the new arrivals were soon spending plenty of time with Striker and Cimarron Smith.

The newly formed bunch had been planning a railroad job when Ryan Freeman rode in and shot Smith dead. Later, Striker had been coldly planning his revenge when the battered Cobb staggered across to his table at the Bird Cage — and one of the first pieces of information the man delivered concerned the size of the payout old man Freeman was due for his cattle.

The outcome of that conversation saw a swift change in plans when Striker immediately saw how he could lift that huge payroll and square accounts with the Freemans at the one time.

All had gone as planned but for the

fact that the Freeman brothers were likely still alive, due to the fact that the father had shown up before they could be finished off in the alley where they'd been waylaid by the four hellions.

Striker had accounted for the rancher though, and felt satisfied that the debt from Wolflock had been erased. Lee had wanted to go back and rescue Cobb when the man was gunned down in the back street but the killer wouldn't risk his neck over some no-account bum he'd known but a short time. And while they had wrangled briefly in those hair-raising moments, men had begun boiling into the streets from the dives and they'd had no option but to gallop off, leaving Cobb to his fate.

Striker's lip curled with contempt. It wasn't the right time to confront Slinger Lee now, he acknowledged reluctantly. But that time would surely come. He liked to have time to work himself up to that pitch of lethal intensity when he knew himself to be invincible — and there were graves studded across the South-West to testify to that grim fact of life . . . and death.

So — sure, Lee's time would come.

But not quite yet.

He was all charm and affability as he went to his saddlebags and produced a bottle of fine French cognac. Big Boy's eyes bugged with simple pleasure and even tetchy Slinger Lee began to relax and get into the swing of things over the next hour as Striker played the good host, spinning yarns, telling lies and bragging about old jobs accomplished then speculating on even bigger ones ahead.

Easy rapport had been fully restored by midnight when Striker suddenly announced he was beat and started off with a blanket over one shoulder.

'Hey, boss,' yelled Magee, 'we still got a little of this stuff left. Where you going?'

'No more for me,' Striker's voice called back as the gloom claimed him. 'I'm posting myself lookout on the knoll. You boys finish her off.'

The two looked at one another quizzically. Then Lee held out his pannikin and Magee filled it to the brim. The big man topped up his own tankard and they clanked the cups together and drank to good times and big money.

★ ★ ★

It was the hour before dawn when Slinger Lee was awakened by Striker's hand on his shoulder. He sat up sharply, knuckling his eyes.

'Shake a leg, pard,' Striker grinned. 'We got to be on the trail by first light.'

As Lee got to his feet and stretched muscular arms above his head, Striker roused Magee with some difficulty. Eventually Big Boy worked out who and where he was, and stumbled across to the fire.

Striker had breakfast already fixed and the three hunkered down and ate heartily, swamping down the flap jacks with scalding drafts of black coffee.

'Gee, boss,' Magee said around a jawful, 'you musta been up all night to get all this done by now?'

'Oh, I dozed some up there on the ridge. But I never sleep much, on the prod. Too scared I'll wake one time and find a posse hanging me out to dry, I guess.'

He was smiling and affable, the testiness of the night completely gone. He threw the dregs of his coffee on to the little fire with an air of finality.

'The horses are ready,' he stated. 'We'll pack up quick smart and get riding. By sundown tomorrow night I want to be a hundred miles to the south of Clantonville.'

It was but the work of minutes to break camp.

Striker and Lee saddled the horses while Magee doused the fire and repacked the saddlebags. From the secluded hollow where they had made their camp, they rode out in Indian file until they had cleared the timber, and the great Clermont Valley lay before them in the grey morning.

Striker gigged his mount into a run and the others followed suit, Big Boy's massive horse managing to keep pace despite the load it was forced to carry.

So they rode through the day. Frequently upon reaching high ground, Striker would call a halt and then spend patient minutes scanning their back trail, head cocked to one side and sitting his saddle as motionless as one of the stone monuments that dotted the valley here.

His new henchmen were duly impressed even while chafing at the delay. Afterwards, Striker would lead them on, their cayuses eating up the miles to their first stopping place, something Striker referred to as Bo Rangle's stud.

The two noted that even as they loped across the sweeping flatlands and low hill formations, Striker continually hipped around in his saddle to check up on the way they'd come.

The two were unaware that during

his nightlong vigil their new compadre had spotted the far distant glow of a campfire on their backtrail. To the killer that meant but one thing. One man or maybe many were coming after them. The bullet that had snuffed out old Freeman's life like a candle would guarantee that some at least were unlikely to quit this manhunt in a hurry.

They also understood only too plainly that, if caught, all three would swing for murder.

6

Killers' Tracks

The brothers examined the blackened remains of the outlaws' campfire.

Matt glanced up at the sun. He calculated it to be an hour before noon. He figured Striker's bunch had broken camp before daybreak, which would give them a good seven to eight hours' lead.

'Looks like they had themselves quite a party last night,' remarked Ryan, holding up an empty bottle. 'Celebrating what they did in Clantonville, no doubt.' He hurled the bottle from him angrily to smash amongst a nest of grey stones. 'Let's push on, we got a heap of riding to do.'

They followed the tracks through the timber then put the horses to the lope upon reaching open country again.

Both men were sitting class horses bred to run both fast and far. Matt missed the runty sorrel pony he had ridden every day over recent months. But that mount had been in no shape for a gruelling test of stamina such as this, having just completed a 500-mile trail drive from South Texas.

His brother on the other hand was delighted with his mount. To Ryan, a horse was simply a means of transport to get you where you wanted to go, and this big bay bronc was doing that job as well as any he'd ever forked.

They covered twenty swift miles before being forced to halt and spell the horses.

Stiff-legged and sweating, Ryan crossed to where the hoof marks of three fast-travelling horses had cut deep into the earth. He beckoned Matt across.

'You're the sign reader in the family. What do make of this sign?'

Matt examined the prints briefly then straightened. 'They're flogging them hard, maybe too hard. One is already slowing down some.' His dark brows knitted in a puzzled frown. 'What's got me boxed, is why trailwise riders like this bunch would run their mounts into the ground. That over-loaded one will be lucky to make another fifty miles, the way I figure.'

Ryan massaged the back of his neck, studying his brother thoughtfully.

'Yeah . . . why?' he mused. Then, 'By tarnation, that must be it! They've gotta have plans to get fresh mounts some-place, so they don't give a damn if these hosses drop dead as long as they carry them as far as they need to go to their replacements.'

Matt's fingers were busy rolling a quirley as he stared thoughtfully into the distance. Suddenly he snapped his fingers.

'Bo Rangle's stud!' he exclaimed.

'Huh?'

Matt hunkered down with a short pointed stick and commenced sketch-ing the outline of a map in the earth.

'It figures,' he said confidently. 'From what we picked up in Clantonville, we believe Striker hangs his hat in Mexico, somewhere around San Rio. He's loaded with money right now and is running south-west as hard as he can lick — or leastways that's how it looks. Between Storytown and the Heartbreak Desert, there's only the one outfit that raises blood horses, and that is Bo Rangle's stud. I stopped by there with Dad once years back, and that man has some of the finest stock you ever saw grazing his acres, dray though they might be. I reckon that's where the killers are making.'

'You could be right, I guess.' Ryan's brow rutted. 'But would Rangle sell mounts to outlaws?'

'He mightn't even figure them to be on the dodge. He's an old man now, doesn't get around much any more.'

'But a place like that — mightn't he have hands who could be likely to recognize Striker from the wanted dodgers? Wouldn't that butchering scum be taking some kind of risk?'

'Well, I know old Bo would never deal with a man he knew to be crooked . . . ' Matt's brow was creased with concern now as he turned to his brother. 'You know, if Bo won't sell, Striker will take. And we don't need to be told what that could mean . . . '

His brother gave a grim nod of understanding and together they strode swiftly to the horses and swung up.

★　★　★

The manhunters loped along the homestead road which was flanked on both sides by high, white-painted wooden fences. Beyond the fences, proud, glossy-coated mares watched their passing as frisky foals kept pace with the riders.

With rough trails in back of them, the Freemans were amazed by the quality of the horse ranch's well-irrigated acres out here in the semi-arid country so close to the desert.

But it would take more than implausibly verdant surroundings to divert them, and by the time they reached the headquarters they were again focused on just the one thing. The man who'd murdered their father.

They reined in at the building whose white-painted expanse contrasted sharply with a heavy backdrop of massive oaks and cedars. The ramrod stood waiting for them on the front gallery as they reined leg-weary horses to a halt.

The man remembered Matt, greeted him warmly, then conducted them inside to the door of Rangle's study, where he knocked then opened.

'Just go right in, boys, we told Bo to expect company.'

Before the cold fireplace sat a giant of a man with an enormous red face and a mane of silver hair. His right arm was held in a sling and they saw bruising on his face as they shook hands.

'Matt Freeman! Great to see you again, boy. And this other young fella is . . . ?'

'My brother Ryan,' Matt said proudly. 'Ryan, Dad's friend, Bo Rangle.'

'Felicitations,' the rancher said grimly. He nodded. 'Yes, the black news got here ahead of you. About your dad, I mean. Worst news I heard in years.'

'How'd you get to hear so fast, Bo?' Matt queried.

The rancher indicated his shoulder. 'From the horse's mouth . . . or more correctly, the killer's.'

'You mean — ?'

'Striker's been and gone,' the man informed grimly. He tapped his shoulder. 'Gave me this, so he did. Of course, he took us by surprise and by the time I realized he had come here for horses he didn't mean to pay for, why, we were looking down gun barrels. I was so mad I grabbed up a chair and he winged me.' The silver head shook. 'Guess I was lucky not to get killed.'

'Real lucky,' Ryan said, and his face was tight. 'So, we're guessing they got away with what they came for, then?'

A maid brought food and coffee at

that point, and while the brothers ate, the breeder told them the story.

'I'll be brief, boys. It was around ten last night and I was sitting here reading when the dogs started acting up. I called Billy to go see what in tarnation was going on, when the door opened and as bold as you please in walked these three hellions. The tall rooster with the eyes of a he-skunk didn't waste time. He just pulled his iron, walked straight up to me and said 'I'm Striker' — just like that — like he was real proud of the fact. Maybe he expected me to die of fright, or something. All I said was, 'I won't hold that against you, son.' But he wasn't going to let me rile him, no sir. He told me straight-out what he had come for. The best saddle horses on the place. Naturally I told him to go straight to hell.'

The rancher paused to select a cigar from an ornate box at his elbow, lighted up and continued.

'Just at that point, my boys came

rushing in. That didn't faze this geezer. He just bailed them up, told them what he'd told me, and promised to blow my brains out if they didn't do what he wanted right smart. He meant it, they could tell he did, so they went and got him the horses and even switched the saddles for them.'

'So, how come you got shot?' Ryan wanted to know.

'See that desk. I always keep a gun in there with the drawer open. These bastards were getting kind of comfortable and swilling down my whiskey, so I decided to take a chance. But that killer's got eyes in the back of his head. He saw what I was trying to do, let me have one in the shoulder and then they hightailed and were gone in a flash, even that one they called Magee, who's the size of a house.'

The brothers rose together.

'Sorry about what you've been through,' Ryan said grimly. He took out his billfold. 'We want to buy two top remounts, Mr Rangle. We mean to run down Dad's killers if it takes a year, so — '

'You can have your horses but you won't be paying one dime, boys,' the breeder cut in, heaving himself erect. 'I'll give you two of the best I've got to see your dad avenged ... ' His eyes twinkled. 'You see, I told that killer he was getting my very best, but I was lying.' He signalled to a hand. 'Frank, go get the Dunsdown colts — and saddle them up for Eli Freeman's boys!'

Within minutes the brothers were seated astride two long-legged duns before the lamplit front gallery where the rancher and his crew stood lined up to wish them Godspeed.

They wheeled the thoroughbreds away, loped off through the gates and then gave them their heads to clear the ranch and picked up the southwest trail.

7

The Dead Man Pointed West

A rifle shot carries a long way on the still night air.

Taking a brief spell on a hill crest, Matt Freeman had spotted a sly rattler edging towards the tethered horses. Quietly he instructed Ryan to hold the animals steady, then lifted his Winchester and fired, the heavy slug exploding the reptile's small skull.

The crash of the Winchester reverberated far out across the moon-washed prairie to be dimly heard atop a lonesome ridge miles to the southwest where the desert began.

The only sound the killers heard was a faint report. Big Boy Magee turned to Slinger Lee with a question in his brute eyes. Lee was staring along their backtrail with eyes narrowed as though attempting to project his vision through the long miles across the night to glimpse whoever it was who had touched off that ghostly shot.

Striker gave no sign he had heard anything. He was engaged in repairing a broken cinch strap, sure hands working swiftly and dexterously, his expression blank.

Big Boy finally said, 'Who do you figure that was, pard?'

'Termites, big feller. Them desert termites are likely the noisiest critter in all creation — apart from the big-footed earwig, that is.'

'Huh?'

That was the drawback in trying to joke with the big man, Lee reflected. Big Boy simply never caught on.

So the lean gunman played it straight. 'Well, it was a rifle and not a six-shooter — that's for sure. Could be some wolver close by, or maybe even a miner somewhere far off in the hills. It's hard to figure distances out here at times.'

'Uh-huh.' Magee accepted this. 'So, I guess whatever it was, it ain't got nothing to do with us, huh?' He turned his head. 'That the way you figure, boss man?'

Striker put the finishing touches to his job of work before getting to his feet. He didn't look at them but instead stood gazing back over their backtrail which was studded by dark clumps of bristle brush and patches of wolf grass. When he spoke, his tone was indifferent, casual.

'Why, if I had to bet money, I'd bet it was those jokers who've been trailing us.'

Magee uttered a surprised oath, and Lee swung sharply on Striker.

'What jokers?' he said sharply. 'You saying there is somebody on our trail?'

The killer swung to face him, arms spread wide and with palms upwards.

'Why, Slinger old pard,' he grinned, 'of course there are. Hell! I thought you knew, otherwise I'd have spoke up before.'

'Damn you, Striker!' the broad-chested outlaw snarled. 'You bloody-well knew we didn't know anything of the sort. How long have you known?'

'Since the first night out,' Striker conceded with just the ghost of a smile. 'I spotted their campfire then.'

Lee bit back an angry retort.

'Then I reckon we'd best prod on,' he muttered, grabbing up his saddle and making for the remuda.

'Sure. No sense in hanging around with trouble in the air,' agreed Striker, his glance following his henchman's receding figure. In the shadow of his hatbrim, the killer's small, wide-set eyes glittered cold, even as he smiled. He had long learned how to appear unconcerned and calm even when emotion gripped his guts. Ever since the night Lee had stood up to him, venom had built up in Striker. He enjoyed the emotion, fed it and encouraged it deliberately. Every minor incident such as this one, was fuel to the flame. Times like this he felt a thrill, knowing he must shortly kill again. 'Soon, Slinger, soon,' he thought.

And it felt good.

They mounted up to leave the nameless mesa swiftly behind. Trees were fewer and here and there now were to be seen occasional mesquite shrub or a blooming ocotillo, certain signs they were striking ever deeper into the true desert country known as the Heartbreak.

As always, Striker rode ahead, breaking trail, followed by Magee with Lee bringing up the rear.

They halted at daybreak for a brief feed. Hot coffee and cold jerky were consumed almost in silence. There was mostly silence amongst the killers during recent days, with Striker continuously preoccupied with selecting the best routes and keeping watch on their backtrail.

The further they travelled the more Slinger Lee's mood darkened, and he focused his silent hostility exclusively upon their leader. A man more accustomed to cutting his own trails and making his own decisions, Lee, in his reflective moments, was puzzled why Striker appeared increasingly to go out of his way to rile him or cut him down to size. Naturally he had no way of knowing the mankiller sooner or later came to treat everyone that way. It was the way he was made, how he operated.

Big Boy Magee, genial enough when not exploding into mindless violence, was vaguely aware of the increasing tension between his henchmen. But sensing Striker already thought him a fool, he kept silent. But how long Big Boy would prove able to keep his thoughts and resentments bottled up there was no figuring. For apart from Striker's abrasive manner, there was the desert now. Deserts had always unsettled the giant, and the more restless he grew the more likely he was to erupt into sudden violence.

Swinging into their saddles they rode on with the rapidly strengthening sun at their backs.

They were in the real desert now. The Heartbreak with its tumbling, tawny harshness and the ever-changing reds, purples and yellows that could lure a man on and challenge him to pit himself against its might in order to prove his manhood, only so often to end up with his bones bleaching in the sun when he failed.

The riders silently drifted by huge thorny cactus, clumps of Spanish dagger and green patches of mescal.

Travelling well ahead now, Striker grinned like a dog wolf, drinking in the desert, luxuriating in its naked harshness. He felt like a king. This cruel country was part of him, was in his blood. Let other men rave about the grassy plains of Texas or the splendour and beauty of the north country. This land was like him, giving little, wanting nothing, yet always hard, vital and very dangerous.

They walked their horses now. Anything faster would be suicidal in this heat. Even with Striker's knowledge of, and affection for the country, they must still needs be travelling slowly and intelligently in order to be certain of making their destination alive.

Just what that destination might be, Striker had as yet not confided to anyone.

Big Boy glanced at the brassy sky, and cursed. He cursed the faraway speck of a turkey buzzard and blasphemed viciously when the rivers of sweat streamed down his big homely face.

He kneed his mount forward to draw level with Lee and the two continued on side by side.

'This here country sure don't buck a man's spirits none,' Magee commented after another silent mile.

Slinger Lee's gaze roved the sandhills. He stared up at the dust eddies and squinted into the blinding glare before finally dropping his gaze to the straight-backed figure riding well ahead.

'It's puking, lousy, coyote country, is

what it is!' he said with real emotion. 'And I still don't know what the Sam Hill we're doing in it.'

Magee produced a dirty bandanna and swabbed fretfully at his jowls.

He said, 'You know, pard, that's just what I been trying to figure. Between us we must know a hundred trails to dodge the law, so why cross a stinking desert?'

Lee said, 'Maybe it ain't the law we are running from?' He paused then continued. 'I mean, think on it. What posse or crack-brained sheriff would hound us like this anyway? You know what I reckon it is — or rather — who? It's gotta be them Freeman jokers looking to catch us up and get square just for blasting their stinking money-bags old daddy!'

Big Boy turned his shaggy head towards him, slow comprehension dawning in his eyes.

'You know, I bet you're right, Slinger. Sure, what else? Well, if that is so, what are we waiting for? Why not hole up someplace, wait for them two to show, then blow their freaking heads off?'

'You know . . . could be I'm not exactly straining at the leash to get at that pair, big fella,' confessed Slinger Lee. 'That joker made mighty quick work of Cimarron Smith back in Wolflock, if you recall. He sure wouldn't be any kind of pushover in a shoot-out.'

Big Boy's brow furrowed convulsively from the strain of prolonged concentration. 'But, hell, that feller's barely just growed. I've seen you bore mebbe five-six genuine fast guns in your time, pard, and then walk away without a crease. What's so special about those rich bums?'

After considering that a spell, Lee shrugged. 'Well, mebbe I'm just getting twitchy in this heat and all. But anyway why run a risk when we don't have to? The way I'm coming to figure, the more times you put your life on the line, the more chances you run of lucking out. One day, some gunslick or other will get lucky, or you might be a split-second slower than usual — next thing, everybody gets drunk at your funeral.'

They rode through another stretch of sun-stricken silence. Accustomed to his partner's cocky arrogance, Big Boy struggled hard to digest Slinger's new cautious attitude, or else gazed distastefully at the landscape. He could not do both at once.

The trail led them along a deep and broad arroyo ravaged and deformed by ancient lava flows. The arroyo lay straight before them, seeming to point with mathematical precision to an enormous distant butte which stood like some mighty totem of the desert lands a great distance ahead.

Even in the late afternoon the heat showed no sign of relenting. Now the horses plodded on, numb and dumb, the riders slumped in their saddles.

For the hundredth time that day, Magee looked at that burnt-out sky and cursed.

'Well, I don't know about you,

Slinger, but I've had me a bellyful of this. It's all right for Striker, this is his country. But what do we want to go riding to Socorro for? It's still a long ways off. Another thing. I'm getting powerful sick of that geezer's sneery jokes and top-lofty ways. Why don't we split up and strike off for Texas on a different route . . . one with trees and water? Leave him to his lousy desert if that's what he wants. It's his neck.'

Lee considered.

He noted that Striker rode easily and comfortably despite the conditions, although his once flash boots were now cracked and chipped, his sombrero greasy and ragged. It was significant that regardless of all other signs of dusting and weathering, Striker's six-gun, holster and shell-belt were well oiled and gleaming.

Lee's stare bored into Striker's back.

He'd been happy enough to link up with the killer back in Wolflock, had even been willing to go along with his plan to get square with the cattlemen who'd killed his pard in that rough town.

Clantonville had provided an unexpected bonanza when they got a scent of the big money involved in the Freemans' cattle sale there. Overnight, Striker had decided to go for the big dinero and worry about vengeance only if it worked in with their planned robbery.

As it played out, they'd only got to blast the old man that night after jumping the brothers with the satchel whom they were forced to club unconscious rather than risk gunfire. Afterwards, Striker acted like he didn't give a damn about the Freeman brothers one way or another. He had struck the bonanza and was content.

Lee pondered. Maybe Big Boy was right. Maybe tonight could be as good a time to make the break as any.

'All right,' he said at length. 'When we make camp I'll tell him to divvy the haul and we'll part trails. Suit?'

Magee beamed. 'We could be in

Socorro by the week's end, Slinger boy.
Just think . . . wine, soft beds, women,
song — and no freaking Striker!'

'I'm thinking, Big Boy, believe me,
I'm thinking!'

Half a mile ahead with a fresh
cheroot going, Striker was wondering if
maybe he really did possess extra
powers, as he often suspected. His
reason for thinking that way was that,
right now, he believed he could actually
feel the weight of their hostility and
sensed things building to a climax.

Them against him. It had to happen
sooner or later. It always did, with him.
No matter what breed of liaison,
association or partnership might get to
involve a man named Striker, it
invariably ended badly.

And he always came out on top and
laughing. Why? The killer would be
genuinely surprised ever to have that
query directed his way. Why was he a
perennial winner? Because he was
Striker, of course. That said it all!

His crooked smile faded and the

moment of ego was thrust aside as he focused, not on the general but rather on this specific situation involving these two particular hellions whose value to him was no more.

The truth was the only reason he'd allowed the pair to stay with him even this long had been dictated by plain horse sense.

For following the robbery, he might have had to deal with a huge posse, or maybe another gang coming after his haul. This had not happened, they had made it into the desert more or less without serious trouble, and now Big Boy and Slinger were just dead weight.

He drew his spotted bandanna up over his nose against the dust and realized he could actually feel the eyes drilling holes in his back.

And thought, 'They must reckon a man stupid not to figure what they're thinking . . . but they are making a big mistake. Man! What a mistake!'

No guts and no brains; fatal combination.

Just look at Magee, six feet four and two-seventy pounds — scared silly of a couple of hick cowboys! Lee was no better. Strong as an ox and sudden with a .45, yet coming apart by the hour.

And, of course, neither was halfway smart enough to figure why he'd been letting those horsemen trail us all this way without trying to take them down. For he'd simply been playing the odds where the pursuers were concerned. Had that pair overtaken him at any time he'd planned to leave his henchmen to deal with them while he disappeared.

It had not worked out that way, and soon the killer knew he might have to deal with the brothers personally. He could handle that in his sleep — if he must. But first things first. He had a job to do and he was solid ready to tackle it.

The shadows of riders and horses stretched hugely across the barren landscape as the red sun hung on the rim of the desert, its last rays daubing the ground with eerily-tinted purples and misty yellows. A coyote yelped once to the south then was silent.

Striker hipped around in the saddle, almost laughing at Big Boy's guilty look.

'Good spot up yonder!' he called. 'We'll rest up a spell and grab us some chow!'

The campsite he chose was a broad ledge of almost white stone set flush against the steep cliff face of a crumbling butte. The rock was scarred by countless fires, the spot having served as a favoured campsite with the Apaches across the centuries.

Between slab and cliff trickled a tiny, sweet-watered stream, and Big Boy had his boots off and pants rolled up before the others had even unsaddled, a smile of pure delight animating his brutish face as he lowered his feet into the cold water.

But no smiles from Slinger Lee. The fast gun was tense. It showed in the way he paced to and fro while Striker broke out the cooking gear. He lighted a cigar, threw it away and promptly took out another. Striker smiling knowingly beneath his secret hatbrim in the background.

Then, suddenly, 'Say, Striker, I got a few things on my mind.'

Striker didn't glance up from his chores.

'Why . . . what kind of things would that be, Slinger?'

'Wal, Big Boy and me ain't used to the desert and don't fancy riding across it all the way to Socorro. So we figured it'd be best if we took our cut now and split up. You could keep on south-west like you want to, and we'd make north. That way, we'd sure confuse those rannies tagging us, and they wouldn't know who to chase. Good tactics, huh?'

It was very quiet in the dusk. Striker permitted the silence to drag on a long minute before easing to his feet.

'Good notion, Slinger boy. And like you say . . . it's time . . . sure enough is.'

'Hey, you mean you ain't sore, boss?'

Magee said, relieved. 'We thought you might . . . well, guess I ain't sure what we thought now.'

'Shucks, why wouldn't I go along with the notion, Big Boy? Makes sense, and I'm a sensible kind of feller underneath. Go fetch the satchel and we'll divvy her up right here and now.'

As happy as a child, Magee lumbered away for the harness pile. He gave a thumbs-up to Lee but the fast gun didn't see it. He was watching Striker warily, pleased with the man's response yet not fully convinced by it.

Like a poodle retrieving a stick, Big Boy returned with the black leather satchel and dumped it on the slab before the others. He knelt and snapped open the catches to reveal the tightly packed bundles of banknotes.

'There she be,' he chortled. 'Sure do make a pretty sight, don't they?'

'Much obliged, Big Boy,' Striker said. He spoke with his hat tilted low to prevent their seeing his face clearly. The excitement was mounting and he didn't want it to show. Not yet. 'OK, big fella, go ahead count out your seven thousand five hundred bucks apiece.'

Lee's head snapped up.

'Fifteen thousand for the two of us ain't a third share each of well over thirty thousand!' he rapped.

'Sure enough ain't,' Magee agreed. 'Shucks, even I know that.'

The killing lust had Striker completely in its grip by this. He felt taller, stronger, faster than he'd ever been.

'Heck, boys, I'm sure you'd agree that I planned the job. And it was surely yours truly who stopped old Freeman maybe cutting us down, then afterwards staged the getaway and kept us safe across all those miles. So, I should get the bigger cut. Ain't that only fair, now?'

Slinger Lee backed up with cat-like grace to put space between them, right hand fanning over gun handle, everything about the man radiating menace now.

'What are you trying to pull, Striker?

It was to be a three-way split! We agreed on that!'

Seemingly casual, Striker eased his way upslope to put distance between them. And when he spoke it was like a stranger's voice.

'Take seven-five each or you take nothing!'

His words hung in the air, seemingly for an age. Seconds stalked the eye-locked silence before Slinger Lee nodded slowly as though in acknowledgement of something he'd always sensed might become inevitable.

Then the anger flared, white-hot and uncontrollable. Instantly he slipped into a low crouch with right hand hovering over gunbutt, yet rock steady.

Slinger had courage.

But was he fast enough?

He was about to find out.

'You planned to grab the lot right from the jump, you stinking, double-dealing — '

'Words, Slinger, words!' Striker jeered. 'Anybody can fight with words. But are you really the hot-shot gunslinger you've bragged about so often? Here's your big chance to strut your stuff — gunfighter. Beat me and make yourself rich and famous in about two fast seconds. So, what's holding you — ?'

He broke off as Slinger Lee made his play. His right hand dipped and instantly blurred upwards, filled with gun. But too late. Striker's weapon roared with fierce authority from across the bright little fire and gunflame flared crimson and gold.

The first bullet caught Lee in the chest. The man reeled back in shocked disbelief, the unfired Colt hanging limply at his side. The next shot struck at almost the same spot. He staggered forward and fell dead across the fire with a grinning Striker following him down.

A slight sound behind him.

Striker whirled.

Somehow Big Boy Magee had circled around him from behind during those deafening seconds of murderous gunplay. Striker brought his Colt muzzle whipping around. Too late! Magee charged him down and both crashed heavily to the stone slab, Striker's six-gun jolting from his grasp.

They sprang up as one and Striker swung a vicious blow that exploded on target — Big Boy's jaw. The giant didn't even blink but retaliated with a pile-driver punch that connected with Striker's temple and dropped him in his tracks. Sobbing with grief, Magee ran to haul Lee's body from the flames.

For a moment of despair he sat there with Lee's dead head in his lap, completely overwhelmed by his loss. This brute of a man had made one true friend in his violent lifetime, a friend who had never mocked his size or called him stupid. Lee was a pard, a true friend and a man to ride the river with.

And suddenly now gone.

A vague sound caused Big Boy to whirl. He froze. On both knees ten feet distant, blood streaming from his face, eyes loco, Striker was holding his .45 in both hands and was either snarling or laughing; it was hard to tell which.

Magee leapt erect, face suddenly ashen. He could not believe what he was seeing. He'd thought he'd put Striker down for keeps.

'No . . . no, Striker, we'll make a deal . . . seven-five is fine with me, I'll — '

Striker's gun belched once, twice, three times, each slamming report seemingly louder than the one before in the cold desert air.

'He travels richest who travels alone, Big Boy!' he howled, and when the huge man fell, followed his slowly rolling body with shot after shot until gunhammer clicked on an empty chamber.

It wasn't until his excitement ebbed that Striker heard the distant drum of hoofbeats. He whirled in shock with eyes raking the gloom, his first chilling thought that the brothers had somehow covered an impossible distance to close in.

It was only then that he glimpsed the snapped tie ropes dangling limp from a mesquite and realized Bo Rangle's beautiful horses had snapped their tethers in panic at the gunfire, and now were already fast-fading dots in the far distance.

The killer sagged. This was a savage blow. He'd gone to great lengths to equip himself with remounts he might well need should the Freemans look like catching up, or if some other emergency were to rear its head out here in the hell country. Gone!

For a moment his brain was clouded by the onset of one of his crazy rages. But he fought it back and moved with a forced calm to his saddlebags to draw out his bottle. He swallowed a cupful of fiery spirits at a gulp, saw double for several seconds, then belched and stoppered the bottle.

He was almost calm again as he took stock.

He was unhurt, unencumbered, well-mounted — and he knew the desert. No sign of pursuit, and he was virtually ready to ride.

Inhaling deeply now, he held his right hand out before him, palm downwards. Steady as a rock.

A short time later the killer rode away from Sweet Spring Rock on his good horse with a satchel containing better than thirty thousand dollars.

Before quitting, his twisted mind conceived a reckless final flourish to his night's work.

Close by Lee's fire-blackened corpse he stood a sturdy forked stick erect then packed rocks about its base until it stood unsupported. He then raised the dead man's limp hand and placed it in the fork, arranging it to point westward.

He paused to smile wolfishly at his handiwork. When and if the Freemans showed up, a dead man's hand would point out the trail their quarry had taken.

If that grisly touch of defiance failed to scare them into quitting, then he was no judge of a couple of a rich man's pampered offspring.

8

Brother Against Brother

The Freemans surveyed their completed task in silence. They had scouted the terrain surrounding Sweet Spring Rock to find a spot where the ground was sandy and high enough to remain out of reach of the little stream when in flood. With no other tools but saddle shovels they'd laboriously carved out two shallow graves and laid the stiffened bodies to rest. When they covered the corpses with sandy soil they constructed a solid cairn of boulders over each grave to protect it from scavenging coyote or buzzard. Hatless they stood together while Matt spoke a few simple words over the remains. Turning away in silence they trudged wearily back to their horses, sweat-soaked clothing plastered to weary bodies.

Ryan leaned his arms upon his saddle, forehead resting upon smooth leather. Matt fashioned one of his brown-paper cigarettes and focused narrowed eyes upon the intimidating vastness of the south-west. It was twilight, the clear, crystal-clear twilight that comes only to the desert. The day's heat haze was gone and the red and greenish hues of the slowly darkening landscape were soothing to smarting eyes. From here, the grim line of the Macos Range was but a speck upon the far southern horizon.

Ryan acted exhausted and edgy. They had covered countless miles during the manhunt — in the saddle twenty hours out of twenty-four, only resting briefly to snatch an hour or two's sleep then bolt down a few tasteless vittles before saddling up again. Throughout that day they had slogged across the scorching face of the wasteland smothered in powdery dust, with lips cracked and throats parched.

They were on full alert every moment. Had to be. It was impossible to estimate distances accurately out here, even to guess how many endless miles they might yet be forced to cover. Reality appeared to blur a little for both men from time to time now. And every moment there was the awareness of whom they were up against and how relatively simple it might prove for a man of their quarry's abilities maybe to double back someplace ahead and lie in ambush.

Reality dimmed for Matt Freeman in that long sundown silence and he was exhausted enough to encourage the moment. He was no longer seeing the gaunt and fearsome desert but the Virgin Mountains of home, blue and welcoming against the sky, the sweet scents of grasses coming to him on a breeze. He stood in the heart of cattle country where every man was his friend and did not even carry a six-gun, much less think of ever having to use one. It was only when he saw his father walking towards him in a Texas twilight that he shook his head and returned to reality.

He stared around.

The grim discovery of the bullet-riddled bodies of Lee and Magee had put the final seal on their belief that in Striker they were dealing with the worst of the worst with their deaths a very real and present possibility.

'What next?' Ryan finally grunted.

Matt expelled a thin stream of blue tobacco smoke. 'We push on. Now.'

'Damnation! We can take a decent spell first!' Ryan snapped. 'We'll make far better time tomorrow if we give the mounts some real rest tonight.'

'Striker ain't resting.'

'How do you know? He could be holed up and snoring like a buzz-saw right now.' Ryan paused to stare about at the gloom. 'Then again, he might just as easy be right close, peering at us over the sights of a rifle this very moment . . .'

'Mebbe. But I figure it different. The

sign tells us that the remounts he stole from the ranch got away on him, so now he is just going to have to keep on riding — no frills or tricks — just grind the miles away hoping in the end we will have to give it best and quit. Simple.'

Ryan averted his face slightly as he replied. 'Maybe we've already given up, but just don't realize it yet.'

Matt's eyes snapped. 'What?'

'Great Judas!' Ryan exploded, swinging to face him squarely now. 'Just take a look at us. We're half-starved and tuckered out. We started out with two of the best mounts in the country here, yet now they are worn down to the nub.'

'What are you trying to say?'

'I'm just facing the facts,' Ryan said emotionally. 'We know we're in Striker's country now . . . that he belongs to this goddamned desert. We are fighting that butcher on his home ground and he wanted it that way . . . planned it. We knew he'd grabbed edge on us when he held up Bo Rangle and stole those blood horses. I'll bet good money he'll use his knowledge of the Heartbreak to sucker us into an ambush where we'll be chopped down without seeing a damned thing — without even the chance to slap leather. That is what I am saying!'

'You mean we should quit?' Matt was shocked.

His brother turned his haggard face away quickly, unwilling to meet the other's accusing stare.

'Well, it's a cinch that us ending up out here with the buzzards picking our bones sure isn't going to help Eli any.'

It was quiet for a long moment, graveyard quiet but for the faint sound of the cry of a curlew. Matt was shocked, bordering on disbelief. His brother backing away from trouble? He'd never seen it before, had never expected to do so. But looking back over recent days now he found he must concede that Ryan's original fiery resolution to run Eli's killer to ground to have lost much of its impetus. He was honest enough to admit that he also had faltered and questioned the wisdom of what they were doing more than once himself.

But quit? That wasn't even an option!

'We're pushing on.'

'Damnit but you always were a stubborn cuss! Remember what the marshal said when we were readying to ride out? 'Let the law take care of this killer . . . he'll trip himself up sooner or later . . . his kind always do. Remember?'

Matt moved off and made a pretence of adjusting his horse's girth straps. He was shocked by Ryan's words. When he glanced up his eyes were cold. 'I'm going on, Ryan. You can turn back if you've a mind.'

Ryan whipped off his hat and flung it to the rock slab, enraged by the other's calmness, possibly even feeling betrayed by his own.

'You are like a damned mule when you get your back up, always were. You get an idea into your thick skull and there's no shifting it. Know what? I've a mind to pound some common sense into you — damned if I don't.'

So saying, he lunged towards Matt with big fists bunched . . . then hesitated. Matt stood watching him calmly, face expressionless. In that moment Ryan Freeman's younger and slighter brother looked like a man moulded out of rock, immovable, cold and unflinching. With a curse, Ryan flung away. He retrieved his Stetson and, jamming it viciously on his head, strode across to his head-hanging mount and vaulted into the saddle.

'All right,' he snarled. 'If we're going we might as well get started. Well, move, goddamnit — move!'

'Whatever you say, Ryan.'

★　★　★

Striker rarely slept when riding the owlhoot. A man could get killed that way. Yet that lonesome night far to the south of Sweet Spring Rock, and well on his way to the first town in a hundred miles, Socorro, he was weary enough to do more than cat-nap where he lay stretched out in the lee of a granite outcropping.

Likely he even did drop off for a spell, which was why he cursed when the horse shook its head harness nearby to jolt him awake. It took a moment to get his bearings. He then rose and looked to the east where a faint light showed far out across the dunes. Coming on to sunrise now.

By the time he finished readying for the trail a few minutes later he was fully alert and ready for the long day's ride that would take him to Socorro. He reckoned on an easy day or two there to rest up, then he would head for the Rio Grande and Old Mexico — rich and free.

About to mount, he glanced back-trail. The light was strengthening by the minute and from this high rise in the trail it was possible to see vast distances in this pristine first hour of the new day. The specks of movement didn't register at first, and he was turning back to his saddled mount and taking out his first stogie of the day before something clicked.

He whirled sharply — and there it was. So close to the northern horizon that they were just flyspecks against the bleached sand of the Heartbreak were two tiny dots of movement.

For just a moment, the killer's shoulders sagged. He'd been bedrock certain the Freemans would quit the chase if and when they reached the slaughter scene at Sweet Spring Rock — particularly when they saw the grisly pointer he'd left behind, which had been specifically intended to scare them off, once and for all — not follow him. Any man with half a brain would have surely quit at that point. Wouldn't he?

That was a ragged moment of surprise and uncertainty. Yet next instant he was himself again and thinking as coolly and clearly as ever.

He'd just have to deal with them. There was no way he intended spending the next week or six months sleeping with one eye open wondering if two hicks from Texas might bob up out of the tall and uncut and start blasting.

Striker didn't operate that way.

Instantly he pivoted to stare off at the broken line of ugly black hills stretching across the due south horizon a day's ride away. The grim Macos Range was the perfect place to mount an ambush, and even as he fiercely resented the need to make the detour, he knew he had to do it. His anger showed in the way he strode to the horse and flung himself into the saddle. The first curious ray of sunlight struck him as he kicked away.

★ ★ ★

The brothers rode side by side under a raging sun.

The journey was dreamlike in its silence, with giant cacti drifting by like bizarre monsters from a nightmare. There were buzzards overhead and nests of great snakes, shining and hideously mottled in the sand drifts by the dim trail. The reptiles writhed and hissed as two lathered horses plodded by, heads hanging and tails swishing flies.

The Freemans had often hunted this way dating back to their first experiences with rustler bands from across the Rio Grande . . . the two murderous range wars in the late Sixties . . . the manhunt for the desperado who had abducted their pretty ranch cook — the late desperado.

Like this, yet not quite like it, mused Matt Freeman as the long horse miles fell away behind. There was one thing different. Always, whether hunting for pleasure or chasing hellions, Ryan rode up front. It was the natural thing for him to do, for he was born to lead. Nobody on the spread ever challenged this status, not even father or brother. Dating back a decade it was always left to Ryan to select the trail, make the decisions and deal summarily with any man who questioned his authority.

But not here.

Both today as on that first day after they quit Sweet Spring Rock, the man on the big red horse had lagged behind — not at any great distance, yet behind nonetheless. Naturally Matt noticed yet thought nothing of it. If Ryan didn't feel like breaking trail, he would. The end result would be the same no matter what the order of travel. Justice would be done and revenge taken.

It was twenty-four brutal hours since the brothers realized the killer was not making for Socorro as they'd figured, but instead had suddenly veered off the faint trace of the Old South-West Trail to push due south. And due south on this route lay the harsh outline of the Macos Range. The brothers reined in and traded stares. The desert could be bad enough as they knew only too well. But the Macos, that unique ugly eruption of mountain, canyon, cliff and jungle reaching some ten miles across the landscape, briefly had a notoriety all their own. Macos Range was a stone and brush 'island' in a sea of burning sand. Thrown up in ancient times by some eruption of the underworld, it was always ugly and hostile but had one small but vital asset which made it unique in this grim landscape. For as the molten rocks had slowly cooled and hardened, a tiny fissure opened at the base of the mid-range sector and the smallest of small streams trickled forth.

As a consequence, the range was now home to a type of almost jungle-like vegetation, offered sanctuary of a kind to various species of birds, animals and reptiles. And, of course, mankind — that was if the alien breed of losers, fugitives and mad-eyed loners you might encounter there from time to time actually rated that classification. No sensible man ever went within miles of this landmark in the desert unless driven there by desperate need of water. The Macos were not known as the

'Hills of Bones' without good reason.

They studied the fading sign yet again. No doubt about it, the Macos was the killer's destination now.

'No!' Matt heard himself say sharply as Ryan made to speak.

'I wasn't about to say anything,' his brother lied, staring off at that tumbled, haunted harshness fanging the skyline. He geared up his courage and gigged his mount forward. 'You star-gazing or coming?'

Matt's smile was brief. He'd thought their journey brutal before but sensed it might seem like easy street compared to whatever lay ahead.

★ ★ ★

Striker rode alone, the way he liked it. He also liked the Macos. The outcropping had saved his life before when the law or deadly enemies of one stripe or another had driven him to seek refuge in the desert lands. He knew the Macos Range was a haunted place filled with mystery and evil, yet the killer pushed his horse through its increasingly vegetated outer fringes as seemingly unconcerned as an honest citizen en route to a church social.

But that was just a front. There was a stink of death here that he found both a warning and a thrill, a reaction he suspected he shared with few others. He set a stogie alight and indulged in a moment's regret. He now reckoned he should have hung back and finished those rich scum dogging his tracks. He'd had his chances, hadn't seized them. But maybe he was being too hard on himself? he reflected. That grisly warning he had left behind at Sweet Spring Rock would surely have deterred most. The fact the Freemans had not chosen to heed it was still a mystery. From time to time today he had looked back and kept being surprised to glimpse those tiny specks of movement far back across the dunes.

He looked again. They were there now. A sneer twisted his lips. It didn't signify one way or another, really. The Hills of Bones provided a perfect opportunity for killing, and he knew this devil's outpost like the back of his hand.

This was Striker country and would save him yet again.

Abruptly he reefed his horse to a sudden halt, his whole frame tensing.

Something was not quite right here in the eerie gloom of grotesque trees and thorn brush. A sound from behind! His Frontiersman Colt filled his hand ... and a gaunt jackrabbit scurried away and vanished down a hollow.

He rode on slowly, a little peeved by his unusual tension. Of course a man expected to be anything except fully relaxed any place in the Macos. That was only natural. Yet something extra was fraying his nerve ends and he couldn't put a name to it.

Abruptly he jerked the horse around and rode back to a clump of Spanish dagger. He stared at it, then grunted. His eagle eye had seen something unusual there, but it had been slow registering. It was a single strand of horse hair snagged to a tiny spike, one brown strand that had not yet curled in the heat.

A horseman had passed by here and not very long ago! So — he didn't have Macos Range to himself!

He circled the Spanish dagger with eyes upon the ground. He saw nothing. The earth here was too stony to show sign. He circled wider and wider in the singing heat with cicadas rasping in their carping monotone. It was not until his ever-widening circle took him through a clump of spiky brush to sight a sandy depression the size of a sombrero that he halted. Staring down he saw the faint outline of a single hoof that was barely visible to the eye. With the bridle looped over one arm he walked slowly back along the horseman's almost invisible trail. This eventually led to another wider area in which he saw where the horse had crossed into a broad sandy shale and where other hoof prints joined the sign. It proved the work of mere minutes for him to figure the number and condition of the horsemen.

'Three of them, two mounted and one leading,' he muttered aloud. 'Desert rats for sure . . . living rough, likely hiding out from the law — ' He broke off with a wolf grin as he stared around with eyes like bullets.

'Three ragged-assed bums likely praying that God will forgive them their sins and send along some sucker packing a whole sack of cash money . . . '

He slapped the fat black satchel strapped to his saddle and the horse pricked its ears.

'Well, they're going to find out that three is definitely a crowd. If those rich man's offspring are loco enough to trail me here, then I can't have Macos bums cluttering up my game . . . ' He swung up and made a point of sitting his saddle with apparent casualness as he continued on through alternating

157

patches of sunlight and deep shadow.

'Either you're getting jittery in your old age, Striker . . . ' he muttered to himself a short time later. 'But it's just like you really can feel beady eyes peering down on you right now . . . '

He was right.

★   ★   ★

The burning sun hammered Kruger's back as he watched the lone rider below.

A grey little butcher in garb deeply stained by time and the desert, the small figure could have easily been mistaken for a clump of strangely formed rock or desert growth, so naturally did he blend with the harsh surrounds. His shapeless hat was thrust back from a low brow revealing a mass of reddish hair which tufted out over bat ears.

Kruger was excited. Hard times had dominated the Macos scum of late but this cocky-looking rider brought promise of improving times . . . and he sure liked the look of that dusty black satchel.

'A sight for sore eyes, to be sure,' he said aloud, and movement stirred in the growth close by.

Konomo, the one-eyed breed, crawled into sight scratching his Navajo navel. He glanced back at the three scrawny horses tethered in the draw, then turned back to Kruger.

'Why the hell do you figure a geezer like this would want to stop by here?' he asked suspiciously.

'Who can say? Nice pony he rides though, did you notice?'

Konomo's evil eye brightened. Of course he'd noticed. Good horseflesh was scarcer than gold here. 'So, when do we jump him?'

'Tonight, when he makes camp.' No hesitation here. The losers had been doing it tougher than ever of late. They lived little better than wild animals here, and no traveller had chanced to come by in too long.

'Good. Our need is great. Ponies on last legs. It is this place. Dark gods live here. Konomo not live long either unless — '

'Quit griping. This is bonanza time, 'breed.' He licked his lips. 'A good-looking horse, some chow, guns and bullets. And that there black satchel sure looks mighty interesting — '

'OK, OK!' a voice interrupted from lower down. 'C'mon, we'll tag the son of a bitch.'

Kruger took one last glance down then, rising stiffly, limped off down the steep animal pad. Konomo grunted and followed.

Three-hundred pound Blitt stood holding their ragged mounts when the two reached the lower level. The two wasted no time acquainting their partner with the good news. They mounted up and pushed off through an avenue of twisted black trees and long vines. They rode easily enough but no man ever really grew comfortable here in this haunted aberration of nature known as the Macos Range.

Konomo had accurately figured the path the newcomer was most likely to take. As a consequence the trio was soon dismounted and sprawled out atop an overgrown bluff some thirty feet above a twisted animal pad, when they heard the sounds of a walking horse.

Striker appeared moments later, sitting erect in the saddle with his hat tipped low and smoke drifting from the cigarillo clamped between his teeth. He was softly humming a tune and gave an impression of a man totally at ease in his surroundings.

'A fool!' Konomo said with a happy grin. 'For who but a great fool would ride so in such a place as this? This will be easy!'

'Dumb redskin!' muttered Blitt, swabbing sweat with a vast kerchief. 'Ain't you learned nothing riding with us? That feller ain't stupid, mate — he's cocky. But who would ever be cocky in a place like this? — you might well ask. Well, I'll tell you. It's a feller who must know how to handle himself — and that means trouble!'

Konomo stared. He looked at Kruger, who shrugged. 'Blitt's right,' he conceded reluctantly. 'That pilgrim has got the look sure enough . . . so we gotta take him serious.'

'So . . . how do we go about it?' Konomo wanted to know.

'Well, we kill him, of course,' fat Blitt replied without hesitation. 'Only thing, we go about it mighty careful, is all. C'mon, let's move.'

*　*　*

Darkness came down swiftly across the Macos Range.

It was some time before the first flicker of a campfire glowed far up along Haunted Canyon several hundred yards from the killer's position downstream.

At a silent signal from Kruger the

other two rose and followed him afoot towards the yellow glow. They halted again once inside the canyon proper. It was ghostly here and gloomy with mist. The killers rolled their eyes at one another and fingered their heavy guns. That fire bothered them. It just didn't make sense that a likely-looking rider would be so careless. Yet here he was, acting almost like he was on vacation in some pretty little town with a town sheriff on patrol. Hell! He had even set up a fire as though in invitation to every no-good in miles. It just didn't sit right. But time was moving on and eventually Kruger gave a grunt and led them along the bank of the tiny canyon stream.

There was no reason to do so, but had they looked up at the gloomy slopes climbing into the darkness above they might have glimpsed the grinning face of their intended victim staring down at them.

9

Odds Don't Count

Sprawled like a giant spider atop the brushy ridge, Striker could no longer see or hear the stalking enemy below now, yet knew they were close.

Instinct told him so.

He bellied back from his vantage place with infinite care and without making a sound then scrambled the remainder of the way down to the piney grove where his horse stood waiting in the dark.

The killer uncoiled to full height and stood sniffing the air, every sense attuned to this strange night, excited by what lay ahead but cautious, always cautious when death was in the air.

Two hours earlier he had clearly sensed the danger as he approached the entrance to the butte canyon. So acute were his hunting skills in truth, that he had even smelled them down there at the stream.

He'd given no sign, simply rode on to reach his chosen spot some half-mile up-canyon by the end wall where he'd made camp, with every outward indication of a weary traveller without any sense of danger, with nothing on his mind but a good meal then some blanket time.

As to whom the enemy might be, he had no notion. But he did know the Macos Range was notorious for the scum its isolation attracted here, twenty desert miles from Socorro and the beginning of the southern settled regions.

If he wanted to lure the Freemans into this labyrinth and stage an ambush, then it followed he must first deal with whatever trouble lurked here.

Nailing Striker's a job for an army, not for a couple of white-fingered rich boys . . . and for sure no rock-crawling outlaw is up to the job either . . .

He grinned then straight away settled himself down. Anger fuelled his energies, but a man needed a cool head to survive the killing game.

The moment he'd first sensed danger here he was figuring the counter to it, and immediately recalled the long box canyon that should prove ideal.

The plan would be to lure the enemy into the dead end then cut him off at the mouth from where he would pick him off one by one at his leisure.

Night was close when he reached the canyon and rode its full length, noting its configurations, where it narrowed or widened. He studied every feature, memorizing all he saw.

Halfway down its length where the canyon widened to almost a hundred yards, he nimbly swung down and began collecting brush and sundried sticks, which he used to build a fire, but did not light it right away.

There was another vital job to be done, one he would enjoy.

Unbuckling a saddlebag he extracted

a roll of twine, and from his bedroll extracted a pair of Fort Union blankets.

It was as black as the inside of a cow in the Macos by this time but his fingers worked expertly at their task. Within minutes he had shaped sticks and twine into a structure roughly the size and shape of a man's head and upper body.

He toted the edifice to a boulder a short distance from the set fire and fixed it in an upright position. He then carefully arranged the blankets around it and finally placed his flat-brimmed hat atop it to lend it the last touch of reality.

By this his eyes had fully accustomed to the Stygian gloom. He nodded proudly at the result and his heart began to trot as a faint sound disturbed the inky stillness, from the direction of the mouth.

He could see nothing, yet his ears told him what the sounds were and what had caused them. He could picture the vermin rubbing their hands and reassuring one another just how simple it would be.

They had him trapped! Well . . . figured they had, which was probably almost as good.

Almost.

Automatically he checked out his guns even though both Colt and Winchester were always fully loaded and in perfect condition. From his bag he took a box of .32 shells and stuffed it into a breast pocket.

He stood for a moment facing down-canyon, picturing them waiting as the excitement surged through him. 'Time to get moving,' he murmured.

Striking a match on his thumb nail, he touched the tiny flame to the compressed tumbleweed at the base of the set fire. It caught and burned, slowly at first. It would take several minutes before reaching full blaze by which time he would be in position, some eighty yards up-canyon.

It went swiftly from there.

The darkness proved no handicap to the lithe figure making its way along the canyon wall. He moved swiftly yet with great caution. There was no way of knowing just how close the enemy might be by this. A kicked pebble could bring a lethal lead hail his way in an instant.

When the broken stone monument he'd noted earlier suddenly loomed out of the darkness, he grunted in satisfaction and began to climb. Soon he was in position atop the flattened crest. He spread full length, rifle at the ready, nothing but the whiteness of his wolf grin showing in the enshrouding blackness.

By this time his fire was blazing hotly up-canyon, and casting its dancing glow along littered floor and gnarled walls.

A boot brushed against rock below and Striker heard a low grunt of annoyance. He scrunched lower and felt his heart thudding against his ribs. Now he could hear the pad of stealthy feet and licked his lips as a flicker of firelight touched the first stealthy shape.

He remained motionless for a full

half-minute before warily lifting his head. The third stalker had just passed beneath, his companions preceding him at ten-yard intervals, stealthy as ground snakes.

His head twisted down-canyon. It figured their horses were there someplace. It would likely be smart to take them out of the game first, he decided. Just in case.

Instantly he slid down the time-worn smoothness of the stone formation and slunk off the way they'd come.

His thoughts flickered to the real enemy as he moved swiftly through the darkness. Too bad it wasn't the Freeman brothers here. But he was concentrating fully on the task at hand again by the time he had re-crossed the little stream at the mouth of the canyon and glimpsed the dark outline of the ponies a short distance upslope.

Foot sore, played out and underfed, the animals showed no interest in him and stood dumbly in place as Striker deftly undid their tethers.

'All right, mokes, get moving while you've got the chance. OK, go on — git!'

He was tingling with eagerness as he stood tall, watching the animals ghost away until swallowed by the darkness.

From the protection of a broken boulder a short distance from the untended fire, Kruger turned and peered intently back along the canyon the way they had come. Half-crouched at his side, Konomo finally broke the thick silence.

'What is it?' he grunted.

Kruger's eyes appeared distended as he gazed around. 'Did you hear something just then?'

'Like what?'

'Like some sound, goddamnit!'

Konomo cocked his head, listened, grunted. 'There is nothing to hear.' He blinked his single eye and licked dry lips as he turned to stare across at the massive seated figure of Blitt beyond the bend. 'He heard nothing,' he grunted.

The other scowled in their henchman's direction.

'Mebbe he did, mebbe he didn't . . . '
As jittery as he was for some reason,
Kruger sounded dubious. What was it
about this familiar canyon that had
been making him edgy from the
moment they rode in?

A windy sigh came from close by.
Slumped heavily against a rock, the
gross Blitt was anxious to get on with
the job at hand. Kill the intruder and
grab whatever he had.

He said as much. Kruger checked out
his gun and signalled his agreement. As
one, the three killers rose and advanced
towards the distant campfire.

Kruger began to grin as they closed
in. Suddenly he couldn't understand
why he'd been jittery. Their quarry,
visible now, was plainly no longer
anticipating danger, might well be fast
asleep, sitting there without a move out
of him. And there he'd been convincing
himself they were dogging the wrong
kind of man in the wrong kind of
territory!

One quick bullet, and that handsome

mount would be his. And who could tell? Could be this intruder was loaded . . . might be a prospector toting gold, even?

When they had drawn to within easy distance of the merry campfire, he halted and signalled for his henchmen to get down again.

Konomo inched up to his side. 'This one does not move. Perhaps he sleeps?'

'Or maybe he just up and died . . . looking on the bright side,' murmured the other, lifting rifle to shoulder. 'If he didn't, he soon will.'

With the Winchester barrel resting upon a boulder, the killer took his time. No need for haste here. He drew a careful bead while his companions watched admiringly, for Kruger never missed.

He fired.

The figure didn't move.

The trio stared in disbelief.

'I . . . I hit him . . . I know it!' Kruger gasped. 'Nobody could miss at that range!'

Blitt disagreed. 'You freaking missed!' he accused in sudden panic. 'Quick! Drill another shot into him — and make sure you get the head this time!'

Instantly, Kruger lined up his gun-sights and triggered. A crash of sound, a billow of smoke . . . and the seated figure slowly tumbled over.

As one the killers sprang up and rushed towards the fire.

Lithe Konomo got there first, dropped to one knee at the figure's side, then sprang back with black eyes bulging in disbelief.

'Is not a man! Look!'

His henchmen peered over his shoulder to gape hang-jawed at the strange construction composed of sticks, blankets and twists of wire.

Konomo and Kruger exchanged baffled glances but it was Blitt whose brain gears meshed first. 'Judas Priest! It's a goddamn set-up!' he bawled, hurling his body violently away from the dummy. 'A trap! Take cover and — '

The soft-nosed .32 calibre bullet

chopped off the sentence in the gross killer's last split-second out of eternity. He never heard the shot that killed him, crashing lifeless upon his back with arms and legs akimbo as the coughing voice of a Winchester rifle filled the night again.

'We been sidewinded!' Kruger howled, legs pumping. 'Get under cover!'

Konomo was moving, but nowhere near swiftly enough. A long finger of fire streaked from the darkness to smash into him with sickening force. Hurled back by the impact, he had one moment to consider eternity before the next bullet struck an inch above the ear, dropping him where he stood.

Striker's deft fingers slipped fresh shells into the magazine of his Winchester where he crouched invisible in deep gloom, his icy stare never for a moment leaving the fire-lit scene before him.

'Nice shooting,' he complimented himself. 'I wonder what that geezer would pay right now to be back in a nice cosy jailhouse in Texas . . . ?'

His eyes raked the scene below intently, but of the third man there was now no sign; meantime his horse was rearing wildly and tossed its head in terror, snorting in alarm at the two dead bodies lying in ever-expanding pools of dark blood so close by.

The fire had ceased blazing but big coals still glowed from the black ashes. During the murderous moments the moon had crept above the humpback crests of the Macos bringing almost a soft-edged beauty to the canyon of death below.

Kruger's pain-racked body was growing cramped as he crouched behind the rock that had saved his life when the shooting began. Time had passed — he couldn't figure how long exactly — only knew it seemed far too long for any murdering bastard to be able to wait him out, surely?

Or might the shooter be dead?

He forced himself to concentrate and count up the number of shots fired. He then attempted to recollect if either

Blitt or Konomo had maybe got a shot away. Could be one lucky bullet had king-hit the killer smack between the eyes. That would explain this agonizing silence with no sign of life other than the rearing horse.

The horse!

Maybe he could make it . . .

The audacity of the thought surprised him. He shook his head violently. Too risky.

So he huddled deeper into his foxhole and stayed there motionless until feeling calm again.

Slowly but surely his old outlaw bravado was returning, he realized. Was he a man or a yellow skunk?

He was beginning to feel braver by the moment when without warning a rifle-flash flared from the deepest shadows beneath the beetling overhang and a screaming bullet came searching for him.

He quivered, he shivered. Then recklessly he raised his weapon high and triggered back at the flash.

Instantly an entire chamber load of howling lead raked his position, the final shot in the volley smashing into stone above his head causing rock fragments to shower down on his trembling head and shoulders.

Yet the outlaw grinned, interpreting this mad volley as proof that his tormentor must now be coming to pieces — that he himself was the strong one.

He would let the bastard sweat it out for a time then strike back when least expected!

He felt almost confident for a time . . . until realizing with a sudden jolt something was not quite as it should be.

But what? shouted his mind.

He twisted, stared about him, froze.

He realized that his head and shoulders, which mere moments before had been bathed in silvery moonlight, now lay in shadow!

His head snapped upwards. That lean figure looming wide-legged above him,

Winchester in hand, surely could not be real! Nobody could be that clever, so stealthy! He could not believe it.

He died in a roaring hailstorm of smashing lead — and didn't believe any of it at all.

The echo of the shots grew fainter and fainter until swallowed into silence by the surrounding hills. The moon hung low in the night sky, casting black shadows long and sinister upon this evil land.

Striker stood beneath it as a giant.

10

Showdown

The Freemans reined in and stepped down. Both riders moved about stiffly, flexing their cramped and aching bodies, and savouring the feel of solid ground following interminable hours in the saddle.

They had followed the killer's trail from the desert and well into the foothills of the Macos, pushing their mounts to the limit of their endurance. Now the moon was gone and with the trails too dangerous in full dark, they must wait till first light.

Ryan said, 'We haven't heard any gunplay from higher up in over an hour. So, what do you figure? Maybe those owlhoots we sign-read did us a good turn and finished Striker off for us?'

'Could be,' Matt replied without conviction.

'Well, hell, man, you figure it out. That was some fierce gunplay we heard. The sign says there were at least three hardcases in that bunch trading lead, and even you'd have to allow that three-to-one's mighty heavy odds, even for Striker to handle.'

'I reckon so.'

But Matt didn't say what he really believed, for he was virtually certain that last shot had been fired by the killer's Colt.

Ryan moodily moved about building a fire.

Matt said, 'Maybe we'd better not light that, man. We're still pretty close to where the action was.'

'Heck,' Ryan said mildly, 'don't you figure we have earned us some coffee after that ride we just put in? Besides, I'm convinced Striker's dead and that those drifters would have his horse by this. They're not going to be fretting about us any.'

'Well, OK. But build it over under that slab yonder to cut down the glare. We'll douse it after we brew up.'

Matt attended to the horses then hunkered down to rest.

He was bone-weary yet his mind felt crystal clear, his resolve to hunt the killer to the end stronger than ever.

He could see Ryan silhouetted against the fire. Strange, but of late he appeared to be giving all the orders while Ryan mostly followed them. Nobody back home would believe that without seeing it.

He shook his head, wondering yet again if this brutal journey was eating away at his brother's hitherto unquestionable courage.

He shook his head angrily.

No! He didn't believe that. He would not!

He returned for the fire and forced a grin as the other glanced up.

'Hot joe coming up,' Ryan greeted.

'Thanks, pard,' he responded, guiltily averting his face for fear his expression might reveal his thoughts.

They drank the welcome brew and each man put away a handful of beans. Then they doused the fire and sat yarning in the darkness, just like old times.

It would be another hour before first light, so they spread bedrolls and stretched out. Within minutes Ryan was breathing deeply, his untrimmed fair hair standing out clearly against dark blankets.

Matt lay propped on one elbow, the tip of his cigarette glowing in the dark. His thoughts were on the next day's ride. What might they find? he wondered drowsily. Striker, desert rats . . . or maybe some new danger they didn't even know about?

He flicked the butt away and lay on his back, eyes closing.

'Wonder what happened up there?' he whispered in the night. 'Is that killer dead or alive, I wonder . . . ?'

* * *

Striker was very much alive — and at that very much alive a mere fifty yards distant from the campsite, unblinking eyes drilling down upon the sleeping figures below.

When the killer had quit the canyon he'd scouted briefly for the drifter's ponies only to realize they had gone, likely searching for water.

His thoughts moved swiftly. He had covered little distance that day, having spent valuable time and energy setting up and executing the ambush of the desert rats.

After that — what the Freemans had been doing while he had been occupied with the scum, was a question that had to be answered.

He'd set off to find out after the gunsmoke cleared and had been drifting around warily through the spooky gloom of the Macos night when, unexpectedly, he'd spotted the distant flicker of a fire.

As he closed in warily on the campsite he cast his thoughts ahead

. . . to when his hunters were dead and he was free to move on.

He would make directly for Socorro to rest up a spell before pushing straight on through to the Rio Grande and lose himself in Old Mexico . . . and not even God could find him there.

He wiped everything but the present from his mind when he heard a horse snicker a hundred yards ahead.

Soon he was lying silent and unblinking, watching his enemies. He was relieved to know for certain now there were but two men trailing him. As his eyes grew accustomed to the feeble light, he could faintly make out the banner of Ryan Freeman's yellow hair against the dark of his saddle pillow.

That meant the other still form had to be Matt, the one who had bested him in Wolflock.

Much water had flowed under many a bridge since that hick town . . .

His .45 glittered in his fist, then he grunted and returned the weapon to its holster unfired.

What point in running a risk and maybe getting shot? He knew that Matt Freeman at least could use a Colt like a pro . . . and in that moment he made a decision. Instead of running an unnecessary risk at this late stage of the bloody game, play it smart and simple.

Take the horses and leave the heroes either to starve here or die trying to cross the desert — afoot!

He mulled over the plan without finding a real flaw. Stranded without horses in the hell hole of the Macos, he couldn't see them surviving long. But even if they should come through it somehow, he would be long, long gone from Socorro into the exotic vastnesses of Old Mexico! *Olé*!

Silently he slid back from the ledge and executed a wide semi-circle that brought him around close to the hollow where the horses were tethered. A faint glow showed in the east, and he knew he must act swiftly.

He rippled to his feet and moved silently towards the horses.

'Who, boy, whoa!' he whispered soothingly.

The animals pricked their ears and rolled the whites of their eyes at his dark silhouette.

'Steady there, old fella,' he said softly, reaching out and stroking the neck of the black.

He was expert with horses and had the touch. He had both untied in a matter of seconds without either animal making a sound.

With infinite care the killer led the mounts from the hollow and away. The light was strengthening by the minute and the sleepers could waken any time. Shake a leg, Striker!

Then the bay gelding shook its head and snorted loudly causing the killer to freeze, midstep.

A short distance away, Matt Freeman sat up to glance firstly towards the east then back at the hollow.

The killer's Colt shattered the stillness with its coughing roar.

The bullet whipped inches over

Matt's head. Next instant his gun churned its response, his bullet ripping its way through the deep brush as Ryan leapt to his feet, brandishing his .45 tousle-headed and still half asleep.

'What the hell — ?' he yelled.

'Striker — I caught a glimpse of him,' Matt bawled rushing towards the hollow. 'I . . . I think he's got the horses, goddamnit!'

A slug droned above the crouching killer as he flung a leg across the black. Another shot whipped by his head as he ducked and touched off a shot at the dark figure charging downslope towards him.

But by this time he was mounted with the lead of the second animal looped over his arm.

He leaned low over his mount's neck and raked with spur to send it leaping forward. But the bay reared wildly and the reins were torn from the killer's grasp, burning his flesh.

Instantly Striker swung his Colt at the bay and blasted two shots into the animal at almost point blank range sending it crashing to ground in his wake.

Running hard, Matt snapped off two further shots at the receding horseman until Colt hammer clicked upon empty chamber.

He whirled at the sound of a violent report. Ryan was down on one knee, the smoking Winchester at his shoulder, blasting one quick shot after another at the fleeing target.

A hundred yards distant now, Striker flinched as hot lead whistled perilously close. 'Bastards!' he snarled, and tucked his head in tight. He rode like a madman, zig-zagging wildly but expertly through the brush, spurs bloodily raking horse-hide.

'He's drawing out of range!' Ryan roared, squinting along his gunsights as he stroked the Winchester trigger smoothly again.

Striker cursed viciously as the bullet clipped his shoulder and send him tumbling. He struck the ground on the downslope. The rope lead was still twisted about his wrist and he was dragged brutally by the wild-eyed gelding as it plunged on in total panic.

'You got him!' Matt roared, charging through the brush with fingers working fresh shells into empty chambers as he ran.

Astonishingly, Striker somehow regained his footing to take huge, body jolting strides on the downslope, until able to seize the rope with his free hand and throw his weight back, jamming his boot-heels in harder and deeper with every plunging stride.

High-heeled riding boots gouged angry deep furrows over a further twenty yards before the animal was finally dragged to a haul, eyes rolling, chest heaving from the violent exertion.

Leaking blood and cursing like a mule skinner, Striker momentarily leaned against the sweating animal to catch his breath before leaping astride.

A Colt crashed in the distance as he raked with spur.

Matt continued the pursuit and kept shooting until the weapon ran empty again. He jerked to a halt and impotently watched the distant figure receding swiftly through the thinning timber.

The killer was gone.

Once clear of the woods, Striker swung his horse westward following the slope, grinning and gasping in pain simultaneously as he thundered on. His rig was ripped by trees and brush and exhaustion was niggling now as he ducked beneath clutching branches. Yet he surged on recklessly, leaving the Freemans to watch helplessly from the hillside until he had swung from sight.

Matt remained rooted to the spot for a long time. Then eventually turned and trudged slowly uphill towards camp, fingers automatically reloading the hot .45.

He paused at the hollow to stare bleakly at the dead horse, shot through the head.

'He got away . . . clear away . . . left

us with nothing to ride . . . ' he gasped to his brother standing above.

'He won't last long,' Ryan said confidently. 'He was hit . . . I saw the blood . . . '

'Creased,' Matt insisted, lowering himself to a deadfall. 'He'll survive. His breed always do. They can never be counted dead until an hour after they quit breathing.'

'Well, one thing is certain. We're in no shape to do anything now. We're afoot, and it's to hell and back across the desert to Socorro from here. Looks like we'll just have to lie up here until someone happens along who can take us on home.'

'We're not going home,' Matt said bluntly. 'We will keep on after Striker until we get him.'

'You can't be serious?' Ryan retorted, and Matt just replied, 'You'd best believe it.'

Ryan crossed to him angrily.

'Look, mister,' he said, anger thickening his voice, 'I was letting you run this manhunt on account you seemed to want to do it, and look where it got us. All right, now I'm bossing the show and I say we will wait here until help comes then head on our way to no place but home. We should be counting ourselves damn lucky just to be alive!'

Matt rose, features wooden. 'We are going after Striker,' he stated flatly. 'I'm going to see him dead.'

They stood facing squarely, each sensing the big showdown was finally at hand.

Ryan eventually broke the painful silence, speaking with quiet force, 'I've gone as far as I aim to. I quit.'

'I won't let you quit.'

Ryan's eyes glittered dangerously. 'Sonny, nobody tells Ryan Freeman what to do, and that includes you. Matter of fact, especially you.'

'Ryan, Socorro's under forty miles south-west. Even if he's gone on, we can get mounts and run Striker down, then simply ride on home. Come on, what do you say?'

'You're loco! All you want is Striker's blood and you don't care if it costs us our necks trying to spill it.'

'You are damned right!' Matt shot back, angry now. 'Are you forgetting what he did, damn you? Well?'

He anticipated a heated retort. It didn't come. As had happened before on their odyssey through hell, big Ryan seemed to retreat within himself, broad shoulders slumping. When he spoke his voice did not even sound like his own.

'I reckon Dad meant more to you than to me, and that you meant more to him.'

Matt's shock showed plain. 'What are you talking about, man? You and Eli were always thick . . . '

'Seemed that way, didn't it? But about a year ago, I overheard Dad and Jim Holloway talking about what would happen when Dad was gone, and Jim said, 'I guess Ryan will take over then'. Dad was quiet for a moment, then he said, 'No, somehow I see Matt bossing the outfit when I hang up my spurs'.

Heard him say it clear as day.'

Matt stared blankly. He was stunned. It was about the last thing he ever expected to hear. 'I don't know why he'd say that, Ryan. My guess is he knew you were listening and just said it to trim you down to size some.'

'No, he was talking straight. You see, somehow Dad figured it out that you were the better man. And maybe he was right. Who knows? One thing I know for sure, though. I'm not going after that mad dog any longer . . . not for you or even for God Almighty!'

Matt was silent, troubled by what he had just heard.

He finally spoke.

'You are coming with me, Ryan. I'm not leaving you maybe to die out here . . . or to croak crossing the desert.'

'By glory you're a mule-headed critter, Matt. But hard-nosed as you've gotten to be out here, you are not bossing me this time and if I have to whup you to prove it then I'm ready to do just that.' Ryan loomed over Matt now, big fists clenched at his side, jaw a rock.

'We're quitting the Macos together and we'll stay together!' Matt insisted.

Ryan's fist exploded against his brother's jaw, dropping him on to his back.

'We ain't!' he raged, diving headlong after him, but stopped abruptly and flinched back as he found himself staring into the muzzle of a .45. Keeping the gun levelled, Matt got to his feet, spitting crimson.

Ryan was disbelieving. 'You . . . you'd haul iron on me?'

'I'll fight you, Ryan, but not here and not now. If we beat one another up out here we will likely both end up croaking trying to cross the desert. So we are staying together and going after Striker.'

For a long minute, Ryan studied his brother's hard-set features. He then turned slowly to allow his bitter gaze to take in all the surrounding harshness. He nodded to himself, sensing, fearing now that he might never make it alone.

'OK, boy,' he said with a sudden grin, changing in a flash as his brother had seen him do a thousand times before. 'Put up the hardware. You've made your point.'

Matt's teeth flashed as he holstered the Colt. The brothers shook hands.

'Talking about Dad saying things,' said Matt, 'I often think on what he said to me one day, out by the Seminole. I was trying to decide on some fool thing and he said, 'Son, if you ever ride out to do something you know is right and that has to be done, never ride back until you've finished it'. I've heard him saying that in my head more than once recent.'

So the bad moment was over. Within the hour they had collected some water then picked up the killer's sign which they followed back down out of the hills and out into the arid sands of the Heartbreak once again.

* * *

A man rode into Socorro at sundown. He was lean and gaunt and his torn and blood-stained garb flapped loosely about him as he rode. His chin was down a little and he wore no hat, his face burnt red by the desert heat.

Towners halted to stare. Anyone arriving from the direction this one had come from was rare in sun-stricken Socorro. To the north, east and west of this outpost of 'civilization' lay nothing but desert for upwards of eighty miles.

Puzzled faces watched this one go plodding by on his rubbery-legged mount. Children broke off their games to point at the 'funny man' yet somehow none dared laugh.

The citizens of Socorro were a motley bunch of risk-takers, gamblers, lost souls and the odd go-getter, fugitive and even a few businessmen. The population was rounded out by a few good women, quite a number of the other kind complemented by the predictable sprinkling of gunmen, drift-ers and cold-eyed hardcases from nowhere in particular.

It was one of this latter breed who pulled up real sharp as the horseman went by, stared, blinked, then looked again. Then he said, 'Judas! But I do believe that there is Striker!'

'B'God, it sure enough looks like him . . . er, kind of,' his companion said uncertainly. 'But he's always been an uppity, flashy kind of a dude, ain't he? What you reckon's happened to him?'

The first man stroked his stubbled jaw. 'Looks to me like the desert happened to him, is what.'

The lone horseman followed the street till he reached the square that was the drowsy, sun-stricken heart of this worn-out town.

Here there were shade trees, a battered general store that had been closed ten years and a rickety church that had been closed even longer. A scatter of drab and dusty citizens was abroad on the square but the newcomer seemed to see none of them, his attention focused on the ramshackle building dead ahead bearing the faded legend O'Toole's Saloon on the title board above the low-roofed gallery.

'Man looks like he needs a hand down,' someone remarked as the horseman began to dismount stiffly at the saloon hitch-rail.

'No. That really is Striker,' warned another.

'So? Still looks beat.'

'Could cost you plenty if you tried to help that one, pard.'

'How come?'

'How come? He'd likely bust your arm if you offered, son — that's how come! That man's too proud and cussed to let anyone help him.'

The killer's boots touched ground and he stood leaning against the horse a moment. He straightened and fingered his shoulder. The wound had festered during the journey from the Macos and he needed to have it looked at. But even more urgently, he needed rye whiskey.

Now.

Desire strengthened him and he

straightened up proudly and squared his shoulders before untying his black satchel and toting it off towards the time-worn steps, wincing a little now as he walked.

The batwings flapped open and a diminutive Mexican woman in gaudy saloon clothes threw both hands in the air and cried, 'My little one is hurt. *Arriba, arriba*! Bring him inside and fetch me the whiskey!'

An hour later a barely recognizable Striker emerged from the back rooms of the saloon quarters on the woman's arm. He was bathed, shaved, fitted out in fresh rig and had been greatly strengthened by several rye whiskeys. When he occupied a corner table and picked up a deck of cards, Marita bustled off to the kitchen, bawling orders. The killer set a stogie between his teeth which a hard-faced percenter promptly set alight with the sweep of a vesta.

He'd made it!

Striker smiled with pride, vanity and

relief now. The journey from the range had looked simple enough at the outset but it was the infection that had sorely tested him out, he reflected, shuffling the deck and watching the denizens watching him. For a time there out on that badlands trail he'd been unsure if he were headed north, south or some weird direction he'd never even heard about.

He fingered the shoulder which Marita had cleansed and dressed then checked out the hand he'd just dealt himself. Aces and Eights. Dead Man's Hand. He smiled and leaned back in his chair.

By nightfall the whole ordeal was drifting off into the background of his mind. The robbery, the flight from Clantonville, stealing those horses then losing them again. That pair of stubborn rich Texans had unexpectedly proved the toughest and most persistent challenge encountered in a lifetime on the dodge, he only now conceded. But in the end, just like always, he had come out on top.

Too bad he'd had to leave them alive, he mused. He wasn't worried about them threatening him here, however. There was no way they could cross forty miles of desert heat afoot — and he'd made double sure they were left without horses.

Nonetheless, he knew he would only delay here until fit to ride, then fork leather again. For he could hear Mexico calling — Mexico and the world. There was just no telling how far over thirty grand in cash might take a man.

He slept like a saint that night and Marita didn't waken him with breakfast until mid-morning. The doddering old drunk posing as the town physician had done a good job on his shoulder and he was clean-shaven, dapper and feeling almost chipper as he descended the stairs around midday to see the poker game in progress.

One of the players pushed out a chair for him and he sat down with his first cigar of the day.

'All right, now what are the rules of this here game?' he asked with a big grin.

* * *

As Striker was lowering himself into the padded chair in the cantina, Matt Freeman hunkered down upon a bald knoll overlooking Socorro.

His brother lay stretched full length beside him, the sun glinting on his golden head.

Ryan shielded his eyes from the murderous sun and studied his brother with a look of puzzlement. The faces of both men showed evidence of recent violence. They had not spoken in many hours, not since Ryan had refused to continue the insane walking pace the other was setting, and Matt had been driven to make him keep going, first by threats and then by force.

Ryan was the bigger, stronger and by far the more experienced brawler of the two, yet had eventually been beaten into submission . . . somewhere out in that burning hell-land.

Before the brutal brawl, Matt had set the walking pace at a long and unrelenting stride. Afterwards, he'd upped the ante to a brutal jogging run through sandhills, dusters and blinding sun . . . and Ryan had kept at it only because of the punishment he would take if he again tried to quit.

It was a journey through hell, and yet they were here . . . somehow they'd made it.

Studying Matt in exhausted silence, Ryan was seeing, not a brother but rather some gaunt stranger with Indian hair, startling blue eyes and skinned knuckles.

He looked back over the years to when he, Ryan Freeman, had been king of the ranch — best rider, talker, fighter, drinker, bon vivant and winner of pretty women.

Had that been just a few short months ago — or an eternity? Had it ever really been that way — with Matt happy in the background and him top of the heap? Maybe he'd dreamed it all.

Unaware of his scrutiny, Matt allowed his gaze to play over the parched landscape and the town sprawled below.

When he shifted his weight a little, what remained of his right boot completely collapsed. The other was already ruined, pounded and ripped apart by an incredible feat of endurance that had seen two men, afoot and in high summer, half-walk, half-jog across a stretch of sun-stricken desert that would have tested the mettle of a roadrunner. Studying Matt now, the older brother was reflecting that not even their father with his wide reputation for an iron will and constitution could have accomplished such a feat. He'd hated his kid brother throughout the entire ordeal, yet now all he felt was pride.

After a spell, Matt took out his six-shooter and blew dust from the barrel. The weapon was old but reliable. Just how reliable he supposed he would soon find out.

They'd already glimpsed Striker's played-out mount in the rickety horse yard in back of the town's one and only saloon.

'Don't do it, Matt.'

'Huh?'

Ryan propped himself up on one elbow with no small effort.

'That bastard will kill you, man. Just the way he killed Dad. You're no match for that breed — likely nobody is, I guess. I don't want . . . '

His voice trailed away. Matt was starting off, not listening. Ryan struggled erect, wincing at the pain of his feet — the same pain he knew the other must be feeling. He reached out and clutched Matt by the sleeve.

'Leave go of me, man.'

'Matt, I don't . . . ' Ryan's words dried up. He was staring into a face he barely recognised; hard as sun-dried leather, eyes flat and a jaw like stone.

His hand dropped to his side. He knew when he was wasting his time.

'You know I can't come with you,

Matt.' He said quietly and honestly, while hardly believing he was saying the words. He felt so bad he feared he might be physically ill. Yet he went on. 'You . . . you understand, don't you?'

His brother's response was to reach out and squeeze his upper arm, a gesture that understood all, forgave all.

Matt turned away without speaking and went limping off down the hill for the town.

He was panting by the time he reached the first houses. A glance over his shoulder revealed Ryan standing silhouetted against a sinking sun. He trudged on to reach the plaza where he found himself forced to rest against the rusted iron fence encompassing the church with the wooden cross upon the roof.

His eyes scanned the shadowy square, searching for a face but not finding it.

He could feel the weakness threatening to return to paralyse his limbs. He straightened and was flexing the stiff fingers of his right hand when a fat Mexican came waddling his way, open sandals flapping loudly on the stone pathway.

'*Señor!*' he called.

The man propped. '*Si?*'

'Do you know a man named Striker?'

The fat man went white and studied him warily, sucking on his unlighted stogie.

'Mebbe yes, mebbe no. What is this one to you?'

'Tell him someone wants to see him. Pronto!'

'*Sí, sí*, I understand. Pronto, pronto!'

The man scuttled away, jowls flapping, eyes rolling. Upon reaching the saloon he paused to fan himself with his straw hat, glanced over one shoulder at the lean figure by the church, vanished inside.

The killer sat at a table with three hard-eyed men, playing cards. Striker's slicked-back hair glinted darkly and he was smiling amiably with an unlit stogie jutting from between his teeth.

The fat man waddled across, panting like a grampus.

'Señor Striker.'

Striker didn't glance up.

'Yeah?'

'There . . . there is a man in the plaza. He — he say he wishes to see you.'

The table fell silent. Everyone heard the fat man's words. The silence gradually engulfed the surrounding tables, the bar and eventually the entire place, even though the messenger had not raised his voice.

Someone wishing to see the famous gunman — outside? Even to the ears of an 'innocent' new girl behind the dark bar, this sounded somehow deadly ominous.

Striker felt his blood quicken but characteristically, finished the hand before responding.

'Who is he?'

'I know not, Señor Striker. But somehow I think he plenty dangerous, you bet.'

A pause. Then, 'Tell him I'll be out when I finish this hand.'

The man hastened away and Striker calmly considered his cards.

'Who do you figure it is?' a wide-eyed player finally felt compelled to ask.

'I'll find out after I kill him. Who's betting?'

* * *

It was very quiet in the plaza. The dying sun cast its long shadows all the way across the square where small groups of the scared and the curious were quietly gathering as the whisper spread of pending trouble.

A pigeon fluttered overhead and landed atop the cross upon the church.

Five minutes had passed since Matt had received the killer's message. He moved away from the fence and stood facing O'Toole's Saloon.

'Striker! Get out here or I'll come in there and haul you out!'

Again that hush gripped O'Toole's.

Striker lay down his cards and blew a gust of white tobacco smoke at the dark old rafters.

'Hungry to die,' he drawled, then rose and went across to the long bar to gaze from the window. The moment he sighted the lean figure by the church he stiffened in astonishment.

Freeman? Impossible!

How the hell had he got here? He should be dead. By the looks of him, he wasn't that far from it. This would be too easy!

He pushed out through the doors and went down the steps into the plaza.

Matt's eyes sharpened as the killer came towards him. He limped forward slowly on tattered boots. Within he was a well of exhaustion, yet he'd never felt stronger or more resolute than in the moment he finally faced his father's killer.

Striker moved with silky grace as he came down the saloon steps then stood facing him. Faces were pressed to every window on the square and drinkers emerged warily from the saloon to crowd the porch, to listen to Striker's mocking voice.

'Hi, kid. Tell me, how's your old daddy doing these days?'

'You've got two guns there, killer — use them!'

It was that sudden — no way back for either man. Both grabbed for their guns with blinding speed. Striker's draw was plainly the faster yet as that lethal right hand was whipping six-gun from leather faster than the eye could follow, he seemed to falter.

He'd overlooked his shoulder wound!

Instantly he brought his lightning left hand into play and cleared his second pistol with dazzling speed.

But by this Matt's Colt had reached firing level and its deep-throated roar seemed to shake the square like a thunderclap, sending a flock of doves atop the church into frantic flight.

His first bullet took the killer in the throat. Striker lurched two steps forward, coughing blood yet still fighting to level both his guns. Matt's next bullet took him squarely between the eyes, snapping his head back to stare momentarily stare into the sky before crumpling into the dust like something made of old straw.

'Well, you did it!'

He whirled at the familiar voice sounding close by, and met his brother's pale smile.

'Ryan, you were backing my play . . . after all?'

'Well, what are brothers for, man?'

For a long minute Matt stared into his face, fully understanding now just how much courage it must have taken to do what his brother done.

Then he cleared his throat and said, 'I'll be back in a minute.'

He strode directly past the bloody corpse and mounted the saloon steps, onlookers moving quickly aside to make room.

'Striker had something belonging to me,' he told them, hand on gun handle. 'I'm going in to get it.'

Nobody wanted to argue with a man in this frame of mind . . . who had just shot down the fastest gun Socorro ever saw.

The bartender spoke, 'First door at the top of the stairs, son . . . er, I mean . . . sir.'

He emerged minutes later with the black satchel in his hands.

It was still early evening when two tall horsemen rode out of Socorro, heading south.

★ ★ ★

The welcome home was developing into the biggest event ever seen in that part of the country, for until that day, the giant spread had given both men up for dead.

'Most likely killed by that outlaw they hunted,' was the prevailing notion. Or, 'One day they'll be finding their bones bleached white out in that murderous desert,' so the real pessimists contended.

The brothers' sudden, sun-blackened appearance astride gaunt-ribbed ponies that quiet Sunday morning, bringing with them the news that Eli Freeman's murder had been fully avenged, triggered off the celebration which just grew and grew as the news spread wide throughout Capshaw County.

Although it was likely that everybody was way too excited to note such details, the reality was that during the early hours of the celebrations the heroes of the day both underwent subtle yet significant changes.

For Matt it meant totally discarding the hard-nosed role he'd been forced to adopt during the manhunt through hell.

He no longer needed or desired to lead, nor to be forced to make life-or-death decisions two or three times every day.

Although enjoying the shindig as much as anyone, he grew noticeably quieter as time went by and was more than happy to merge into the background by the time the first stars had begun to wink out over Kingsville Ranch.

The changes in his brother proved exactly the opposite yet equally dramatic.

Uncharacteristically subdued in the first couple of hours, Ryan slowly came out of his unfamiliar shell, then quickly and easily warmed to the acclaim and praise that was heaped upon him . . . whether he sought it or not.

Everyone had at least a sketchy notion of what had transpired up north. Yet although Ryan himself had made no attempt to deny that Matt had taken the killer down, soon enough, people were slapping the older brother on the back and demanding to hear details of the murderous manhunt — from him.

For it had always been that way: Ryan in charge, his quiet brother tagging along.

Eventually Ryan Freeman was sounding just like the hero he'd almost been, and later in the evening when his brother happened to stroll by within earshot with pretty Judy Flynn on his arm, he overheard Ryan saying, ' . . . Well, we had to make a decision in the Macos, so I said to Matt — like it or lump it, man, we've gotta go after that killer afoot across the Heartbreak if we must and make darn sure we get him . . . '

He then broke off abruptly as though sensing something. When he turned to see Matt and the girl, he flushed and grinned awkwardly. 'Heck, Matt, guess I was kind of . . . '

'No, keep going,' Matt grinned. He nodded to the admiring circle. 'I've got to tell you, I wouldn't be standing here with all you fine folks but for my brother, so you should hear him out.'

'You're too modest, Matt Freeman,' smiled pretty Judy, squeezing his arm as they moved off. She had heard the true unadorned story earlier from both brothers. 'By tomorrow the whole county will be talking about how Ryan Freeman saved the money, his brother and anything else worth saving. Surely that isn't right?'

Matt just grinned. He could never expect her to understand fully. The old image of the brothers Freeman, with Ryan up front and in charge, and himself quiet and comfortable in the background and getting things done, had worked for twenty-five years and he was looking forward to twenty-five more of the same.

Jim Holloway, top hand and pard, approached the couple as they halted at the punchbowl. 'Say, Matt, I guess you're kinda tied up, but we got us a good crop of calves while you was away and I reckoned mebbe you'd like to . . . ?' Matt grinned and set his glass aside. 'Lead the way, Jim. Coming, Judy?'

The girl took his arm again and, strolling across the lawns for the barn, Matt Freeman was feeling like the tallest man in Texas.

THE END

We do hope that you have enjoyed reading this large print book.

Did you know that all of our titles are available for purchase?

We publish a wide range of high quality large print books including:
Romances, Mysteries, Classics
General Fiction
Non Fiction and Westerns

Special interest titles available in large print are:
The Little Oxford Dictionary
Music Book, Song Book
Hymn Book, Service Book

Also available from us courtesy of Oxford University Press:
Young Readers' Dictionary
(large print edition)
Young Readers' Thesaurus
(large print edition)

For further information or a free brochure, please contact us at:
Ulverscroft Large Print Books Ltd.,
The Green, Bradgate Road, Anstey,
Leicester, LE7 7FU, England.
Tel: (00 44) **0116 236 4325**
Fax: (00 44) **0116 234 0205**

REMEMBER KETCHELL

Nick Benjamin

The brutal beating from big cattle boss Ethan Amador left cowhand Floyd Ketchell near death: punishment for daring to fall in love with his beautiful daughter, Tara. Now, returning five years later, and a top gunfighter, he wants his revenge. But he finds many changes in the town of Liberty, Texas. Tara, a ranch boss herself, has a handsome hardcase as her right-hand man. Can Ketchell rekindle the fierce passion they had once shared and still kill her father?

MASSACRE AT BLUFF POINT

I. J. Parnham

Ethan Craig has only just started working for Sam Pringle's outfit when Ansel Stark's bandits bushwhack the men at Bluff Point. Ethan's new colleagues are gunned down in cold blood and he vows revenge. But Ethan's manhunt never gets underway — Sheriff Henry Fisher arrests him and he's accused of being a member of the very gang he'd sworn to track down! With nobody believing his innocence and a ruthless bandit to catch, can Ethan ever hope to succeed?

DEATH AT BETHESDA FALLS

Ross Morton

Jim Thorp did not relish this visit to Bethesda Falls. His old sweetheart Anna worked there and he was hunting her brother Clyde, the foreman of the M-bar-W ranch. Her brother is due to wed Ellen, the rancher's daughter. He is also poisoning the old man to hasten the inheritance. Thorp's presence in town starts the downward slide into violence . . . and danger for Anna, Ellen and Thorp himself. It is destined to end in violence and death.

VENGEANCE UNBOUND

Henry Christopher

There are some folk who brand Russell Dane a coward — some believe him to be a murderer. And Dane has many more who want him dead: the man he should have fought in a duel; his own uncle; the town that tried to lynch him, and the outlaws he takes refuge with. With so many out for his blood Dane must learn to handle a Colt and confront his enemies. Will his gun craft keep him alive . . . ?

SHOOT-OUT AT OWL CREEK

Corba Sunman

With a law star in his pocket and a gun in his holster, Kell Bannon rides into the Big Bend country of Texas to set up the Parfitt gang for capture. Prepared for a shoot-out, he faces more trouble with Clarkville's crooked Sheriff Bixby; the aggressive ranch foreman, Piercey; and Mack Jex, boss of the local rustling business. It's tough work, and for Bannon, he knows that only his deadly gun and quick shooting can bring a satisfactory result.

JUDGE COLT PRESIDES

George J. Prescott

When one of the powerful Ducane family is hanged for murder in a border town, his father wipes out the place in revenge. Deputy Federal Marshal Fargo Reilly goes south to dispense justice and becomes involved in a gun-running conspiracy, and a plot to murder the president of Mexico. Reilly and his deputy Matt Crane fight to destroy the gang. But can Reilly also stop them from ransacking the nearby town of Perdition, where *Judge Colt Presides*?